MW00946681

Enjoy every exciting book by Gregory O. Smith

The Wright Cousin Adventures
The Treasure of the Lost Mine
Desert Jeepers
The Secret of the Lost City
The Case of the Missing Princess
Secret Agents Don't Like Broccoli
The Great Submarine Adventure
Take to the Skies
The Wright Cousins Fly Again!
Reach for the Stars
The Sword of Sutherlee
The Secret of Trifid Castle
The Clue in the Missing Plane
The Wright Disguise
The Mystery of Treasure Bay
The Secret of the Sunken Ship
Wright Cousin Adventures Trilogy Sets 1-5

The Wright Cousin Adventures Cookbooks
#1 Fun Cookbook: Sweet Treats that bring a Smile!

Additional Books
Rheebakken 2: Last Stand for Freedom
Strength of the Mountains: A Wilderness Survival Adventure
The Hat, George Washington, and Me!

For all the adventures, visit **GregoryOSmith.com**

"So, what's this Wright Dis-gwisey?" asked Tim.

"It's pronounced *disguise*," Kimberly replied, "and it's our newest adventure."

"Good," said Tim. "I like new adventures. Count me in."

"Okay," said Kimberly, "as long as you don't try to sneak any cartoon drawings onto the cover."

"Cartoon drawings?" said Tim with a smile. "Me? Now sis, what makes you think I would ever do such a thing? Wait a minute, what did you say you did with that cover file?"

"Timothy Wright, don't you dare!" Kimberly sighed. "Brothers!"

The WRIGHT DISGUISE

The WRIGHT DISGUISE

PAINTBALL

Gregory O. Smith

Dedication

To my three patient editors: Lisa Smith, Anne Smith, and Dorothy Smith, and to those who protect girls and women in the world.

Author's Note

When our five children were growing up, we were always on the lookout for good, uplifting books, good adventures and mysteries that we could read with them. When we found a good book, our family—my wife and I and all of our children— would gather around and we would take turns reading aloud. When the weather was warm enough, we would sit in the shade at our big redwood picnic table. The table was under a big live oak tree that was six feet in diameter at the trunk. There was a treehouse nestled in its branches. The tree was hundreds of years old and its branches spread out over a hundred feet. We had an old wooden porch swing hung from one mighty branch and a rope swing from another.

We would sit at the large, comfortable redwood picnic table and read for hours. Sometimes we would read extremely fast because we wanted to find out what happened next in the book. We would read and read and read until the book was done. I wouldn't say we were lost in the book because we were never lost. We were *found* in the book.

Those are memories and fun times we will never forget. The adventures, the humor, and mysteries. The good guys and girls plowing through all kinds of tough things to make the world right and help good win in the end.

I hope you are enjoying the Wright cousins, their friends, and their goodness. They are trying to do good, to be kind, and make a difference. They don't quit, no matter how hard things get. They are reverent toward God and that is so important during these challenging times facing all of us. God, family, country...things worth living for.

Thank you for purchasing and reading my books. If enough people keep doing that, it means the Wright cousins can keep going, keep moving forward, and I can keep writing about their adventures. Please tell other people about them so they can enjoy them, too. Now get ready to join the Wright cousins as they try to discover *THE WRIGHT DISGUISE!*

—Gregory O. Smith

CHAPTER 1

The Test

"Tim, you're wiggling the periscope too much, I can't see," said 17-year-old Robert Wright to his 14-year-old cousin. It didn't help that the dust and smoke were still clearing from the boys' last experiment.

"I'm trying," Tim replied. "It's kind of heavy, you know."

"It should be," said Robert, "it's from Grandpa's old army tank tractor that he uses on his ranch in the mountains."

"What are you doing with it?" asked Tim.

"Repairing it," Robert said. "I'll take it back next time we visit him."

"My turn to look," said Tim, peering through the periscope to view their latest experiment. "Do you think we've got the mixture right this time?"

"We'll find out in just a minute," Robert replied. "In science, we use the scientific method. You never know until you can repeat the experiment over and over and get the same finished product."

"Well, we've been repeating this over and over, but we keep coming up with things that don't work," said Tim, rubbing his slightly singed eyebrow from their last attempt that had mysteriously exploded.

"We're totally being successful," Robert said. "It's like what inventor Thomas Edison said while trying to perfect the incandescent light bulb, 'I have not failed. I've just found 10,000 ways that *won't* work.'"

"Yeah," said Tim, "but our project is due in a few days. We don't have time to find out 10,000 ways that don't work. Our grades are going to get squashed, and my mom and dad don't like squashed grades."

"I don't like them either," Robert replied. "Cucumber grades are much better."

"Cucumber grades?" said Tim.

"Yes," said Robert, "don't be such a pickle. We're going to get this project done, just wait and see. Oh, and be ready to hit the dirt if I say so."

Tim and Robert had on safety goggles and yellow construction hard hats. They were hunkered down behind a plastic table tipped on its side in Tim's backyard. Robert had his arm stretched out over the top of the table, holding a long stick attached to a small glass beaker. Tim was holding the periscope up so Robert could view through it.

"What do you see?" asked Tim.

"It's starting to bubble," Robert replied.

"Is that good?" asked Tim.

"Maybe," said Robert.

Robert tilted the beaker a little more. The long wooden pole he was holding twisted suddenly in his hand, dumping the entire beaker's liquid into the second one.

"It's starting to bubble like crazy," said Tim, peeking over the top of the table. "It's filling up the whole jar."

"Run for it!" shouted Robert. He and Tim dropped their equipment and dashed for the other side of the lawn. They dove behind a bench as a loud **_Kaboom_** shook the air.

They waited a moment before creeping warily over to their science project. There was a small trail of gray smoke rising from a pile of black goo.

"Puey!" said Tim, holding his nose and poking a stick at the goo. "It smells like burnt eggs."

"Probably the sulfur we put in it," Robert replied. "I was hoping it might give it some color."

"This paint stuff is hard to do," said Tim. "Maybe we should have just offered to write poems about chemistry instead."

"We're going to have to do more research," said Robert, poking at the goo with a stick. "Invention is 99% perspiration and 1% inspiration, or something like that."

"Research?" said Tim. "Then we'd better hurry. You look on the internet and I'll check the TV. Wiley E. Coyote, Bugs Bunny, Yosemite Sam, and the Road Runner should have some ideas for us, right?"

*   *   *

The Wright cousins had a mountain of schoolwork to do. They had recently returned from the country of Gütenberg after helping their good friends, princesses Sarina, Katrina, Maria and their father, Alexander Straunsee, king of Gütenberg.

The Wrights had already missed the beginning of Fall semester. The classes had completed their start-of-the-year reviews and were now into solid, new instruction. To make matters worse, Tim and Robert Wright had somehow gotten themselves enrolled in an upper level, advanced chemistry class.

Robert and Tim met with the high school counselor about the class on their first day back.

"It's in room twelve-thirty-four," said Tim, remembering his class schedule.

"Ah, yes, *Advanced Chemistry*," grinned the counselor. "A yearly favorite."

"But we didn't sign up for it," said Robert and Tim at the same time.

"You probably requested it during registration last season. Let's take a look."

The counselor pulled up the boys' schedules on his computer. "Chemistry, yes, you've both got it. There's one problem, though," said the counselor, "it's not with us. We don't have a room twelve-thirty-four. We only go up to 428. It looks like you guys are enrolled in a 300-level class at the college. That's junior level stuff. How did you guys do that?"

"College?" said Tim, looking quizzically at his cousin. "I'm barely a first semester high school freshman. Yes, Robert, how did we do that?"

"Beats me," said Robert. "How do we get the class changed?"

The high school counselor shrugged his shoulders and said, "You'll have to talk with the college."

"But that's a long walk across town from here," said Tim.

After school, Tim and Robert enlisted their moms' help. Each mom chuckled about Tim and Robert being enrolled in an upper level, college chemistry class. But they also saw the grief it was causing their sons, so they dove in to help solve the problem.

Robert's mom, Mrs. Connie Wright, had quickly contacted the college and set up an appointment for that afternoon to get the matter cleared up. Tim and his mom, Mrs. Rebecca Wright, were going, too. They would all ride together in Connie Wright's minivan.

Robert's mom had to quickly finish putting together the dinner she was making for their neighbors, the Ramirez family. The family was sick and she had offered to bring in a meal to help them.

After dropping off the food at the Ramirez's home, the Wrights drove over to the college. Along the way, the Wright moms reminisced about their own college experiences.

"I remember my sophomore year," said Tim's mom, "I was mistakenly given a *D* instead of an *A* on my report card. It took me a month and a meeting with the department head to finally get it corrected. It really stressed-out my Christmas break."

"Ah, yes, those were the days," added Robert's mom, "we had macaroni and cheese or ramen noodles almost every night because we couldn't afford anything else."

"And jogging around the indoor track at the field house is where I met Kevin," said Tim's mom. "We had the same PE class together. It took him three weeks to get up the courage to ask me out for a date."

"Aunt Rebecca, how *did* Uncle Kevin ask you out?" said Robert.

"Well, the whole class was jogging. Your Uncle Kevin got a late start and sprinted to catch up. He tripped on one of his loose shoelaces and fell right in front of me, tripping me, too."

"Dad had loose shoelaces?" asked Tim.

"Yes, and we both went sprawling. It was so embarrassing. There we were, blocking half the track. As other joggers were swerving around us, Kevin blurted out, 'Rebecca, would you please go to the homecoming dance with me?' He looked so distressed, I didn't have the heart to say 'no.' So, of course I said 'yes.' He apologized for tripping me, helped me up, and we started jogging again. We kind of laughed about it and we didn't trip once the rest of the day. We hit it off from there and the rest is history."

The Wrights soon arrived at the town college. Robert, Tim, and their moms met with a college official over enrollment. "How may I help you?" said the counselor.

"There's been a mistake," said Robert's mom, handing the man a copy of Robert's class schedule. "Our boys have accidentally been enrolled in a college course you offer here."

"Let's take a look," said the counselor, sitting down at his desk computer.

It took a moment for the man to locate Tim and Robert in the system. He finally found them by looking at the students enrolled in the chemistry class. "There you are," he said. "How did you two get enrolled in this class? It's for chemistry majors."

"But we didn't enroll in the class," said Robert. "We're not even students here."

"Of course," said the counselor. "According to our records, you have both been skipping class and you've missed two quizzes already. That kind of behavior is not typical of *our* students."

"But we're not even enrolled or accepted by the college yet," said Robert.

"No problem," the counselor replied, "I've got the forms right here."

"You don't understand," said Tim's mom. "These boys have not yet even graduated from high school."

"No problem," said the counselor with a smile, "we have

students do advanced placement work here all the time, though not usually in chemistry. Don't worry, though, I can help get you in."

"But we don't want in," spoke up Tim. "I'm still a minor. I want out."

"Again, no problem," the counselor replied. "We've had many miners study in our excellent geology program here. Did you want to mine for gold ore or for silver ore?"

"I meant minor with an 'o'," corrected Tim.

"Oh, you want to *minor* in geology. That would be fine. You can choose your major later. A lot of people have a tough time making up their minds about their field of study, so they need to experiment around with different classes."

"But Robert and I aren't chemistry people," said Tim. "We're more like 'mad scientists.'"

"Young man, we will have none of that here," the counselor replied. "You may choose to be a scientist or not, but we will not have anybody getting mad or angry around here. That is simply not allowed!"

"Um, sir, could we just drop the class, please?" asked Robert.

"The official drop date was last Tuesday," replied the counselor. "If you boys try to drop now, you'll get a big, ugly UW—Unofficial Withdrawal—on your college records. And believe me, you don't want a UW on your record. It would hurt your college GPA, you'd have to pay back your financial aid, and it would decimate your chances at getting any future scholarships. "No, you mustn't do that."

"No?" said Robert.

"No," said Tim.

The counselor gave the boys access information for the class discussion website and encouraged them to "continue the class they had signed up for."

"But we didn't sign up for it," complained Tim to Robert as they and their moms walked out of the ASB building. Without fully knowing it, Tim and Robert suddenly felt the weight that all college students carry: a ton of homework, tests, and big projects. They had a big project due by the end of the following week.

Squaring his shoulders, Robert realized he was not a newbie to chemistry. After all, he and his friend, Marci Franklin, had helped with the rocketry and fuel mixture calculations during the spaceplane project in their *Reach for the Stars* adventure.

Tim, though, was a different story. He was totally up a creek without a paddle.

"Well, if anybody can do it, you two boys can," Tim's mom said. "Make a plan, break the tasks into manageable pieces, and put your plan to work." Noting Tim's growing distress, she added, "And just think of all the fun you'll have as college students: going to football games, ski trips, dances, dates...wait, you're only fourteen. Forget that. I'm sure Dad would be happy to help you with your homework."

"Mom," said Tim, with a mischievous grin, "now that I'm a college student, can I borrow the family car please?"

CHAPTER 2

Real Class

"Nice try, kiddo," his mom replied. "But do enjoy my homecooked food while you can. When you go to college, you might have to eat cafeteria foods like liver and lima beans."

Tim just held his nose in reply.

After they had gotten back to Robert's house, Robert asked Tim, "So, what kind of project should we do for our exciting college chemistry class?"

"And what does *chemistry* mean again?" said Tim.

"That's an easy one," said Robert's seventeen-year-old twin sister, Lindy, from the other side of the living room, referencing her photographic memory. She was studying an interesting book about the big lodges at different national parks. "*Chemistry* is the branch of science that deals with the properties, composition, and structure of elements and compounds, how they can change, and the energy that is absorbed or released when they change."

"And what does that mean in English?" said Tim.

Lindy grinned and said, "It's what things are made of and how they work together."

"Here's what some of the other students are doing," said Robert, reading from his phone, "Finding the EMF of an Electrochemical Cell, Sterilizing Water by using Bleaching

Powder, The Effect of Potassium Bisulphite as a Food Preservative, Nanoparticle Stained Glass—."

"Nano what?" said Tim.

"Nanoparticle glass," Lindy replied. "It's good for making scratchproof eyeglasses, crack-resistant paints, anti-graffiti coatings for walls, transparent sunscreens, stain-repellent fabrics, self-cleaning windows and ceramic coatings for solar cells."

"Wow, Lindy," said Tim, "could you take this class for me?"

Robert read more from the list. "Reversible Sunglasses, Focused Ion Beams, Liquid Metals..."

"Liquid Metals?" said Tim. "That sounds like some kind of new energy drink."

"No, definitely not," said Robert, continuing, "Stain Resistant Fabric, Chocolate Analysis, Alka-Seltzer Rocket Races, and the Visible Spectra of Soda Pops."

"The chocolate and soda pops doesn't sound so bad," said Tim. "Maybe we could just eat a bunch of candy bars and call it good."

"Sorry, those projects are already taken," said Robert.

"Okay, how about jelly-filled donuts?" asked Tim.

"Eaten," said Robert, "I mean, taken."

"Rats," said Tim. "Hey, I've got a bunch of scratched-up metal toy cars and trucks on one of my shelves back home. Maybe we could make up that kind of paint that changes colors when they get hot. That would be cool on my cars."

"Those are called *thermochromic paints* or *leuco dyes*," added Lindy, still studying her architecture book.

"Like a toy locomotive?" said Tim.

"No, not *loco*," said Lindy with a smile, "*leuco* dyes. Leuco means colorless or white. Leuco dyes are ones that can switch between two chemical forms, usually colorless to a color like blue, black, red, orange, green, or magenta. They can be switched by light, *photochromism*, temperature, *thermochromism*, or pH acidity—*halochromism*. They're used in thermal printers and pH—*potential of hydrogen*—indicators."

"Whew! Now I *totally* think you should take our place in college," said Tim. "You could even give yourself extra credit for teaching the class!"

"Nice try, Timbo," Lindy replied, "but I wouldn't want to spoil all the fun you guys are going to have."

"Fun?" said Tim. "We're still trying to decide what kind of project to do. Lindy, it sounds like you've already done them all."

Lindy grinned and went back to her book, leaving the boys to sort out their project themselves.

"Back to work, Timbo," said Robert.

"Well, what about our broccoli bomb recipe?" asked Tim.

"No can do," said Robert, "that's our Top Secret recipe to protect ourselves and America, remember?"

"Oh yeah," said Tim.

Tim and Robert discussed flying trees, rocket propelled bicycles, standardized peanut butter sandwich making instructions—it must have been lunch time—and more.

Since *necessity*, or, in Tim and Robert's case, *desperation* is the mother of all invention, Robert and Tim finally made their decision: leuco dyes. Their teacher approved the project—as long as they created their own paint formulas—and they went to work. Twenty-eight kabooms later, they were still working on it.

Robert and Tim's college chemistry was a combo class, part online plus two days per week in the actual campus classroom. During the online days, Tim and Robert met in the high school library to work on the class together.

Tuesday, Robert and Tim were to attend their first, in-person Chemistry class. As Tim's mom drove them to the college campus, Tim told Robert and his mom about the dream he'd had the night before.

"We were rushing to school," said Tim. "First, we couldn't find the classroom. When we finally found it, the door was locked. We had to get a custodian to unlock the door for us. He did and left. I tried the door handle and it fell off in my hand. I went to put it back on and the door broke in half. We finally got the door open and walked into the classroom just as the teacher, I mean, professor, was announcing that it was our turn to come up to the front of the class to do our oral report. He looked at us over the top of his glasses and said, 'here they are.' It was crazy."

"We had forgotten about even doing the research, let alone giving a report on it. Robert, you looked at me and said, 'You've got this, Tim, I did the last one.'"

"I'll have to remember that line," said Robert. "That's a good one."

"Wait, no, that's my line," said Tim. "So, Robert, you sat down in the audience and I had to go clear up to the front of the class and onto the stage. I felt like I was going to the guillotine during the French Revolution. I stepped on something. I looked down and saw it was my peanut butter sandwich. Somehow, it had fallen out of my back pocket. The teacher looked at me and told me not to take it off my foot, so I just walked up to the front of the room, with my squished sandwich stuck on the bottom of my shoe, squishing it more and more. It was my favorite kind of peanut butter sandwich, too, made with homemade strawberry jam. I checked my shoelaces to make sure they were tied, like great Aunt Opal always tells me to do, and then I noticed...I was still in my pajamas! It was totally embarrassing!"

"Thank goodness it was just a dream," said Robert.

Robert and Tim located their college chemistry classroom, found some seats, and quickly sat down.

"Today," said the professor, "we will begin your experiment presentations and demonstrations of the scientific method."

Robert and Tim glanced worriedly at each other. They hadn't finished their leuco dye project yet, so they would have to come up with something else.

"Aw, don't worry," whispered Robert, "'Wright' is near the end of the alphabet. The teacher won't call on us today."

"Good," said Tim.

"Robert and Tim Wright," the college professor called out, "two-minute warning. You're next."

"What?" said Robert. He thought for a second and then started desperately digging through his backpack. Tim, this calls for Emergency Plan BBA, okay?"

"What's that?" whispered Tim, making sure his peanut butter sandwich was secure.

"Best British Accent," Robert whispered back. "They'll think we're important foreign visitors. Stiff upper lip and all that, good chap."

"Jolly right," Tim replied, willing to try.

"Thank you for your demonstration," Robert and Tim heard the professor say. "Okay, Robert Wright and Timothy Wright, you're up."

Tim looked down to make sure he wasn't still in his pajamas.

"Okay, *jolly* good," said Robert in a strong British accent. He rose to his feet, looking around at the other students.

"*Jolly* right," said Tim.

Robert and Tim quickly made their way up to the front of

the classroom where the experiment demonstration bench was waiting for them. The boys glanced at each other, took a deep breath, and dove in, desperately hoping that enthusiasm might help carry the day. They donned white science aprons in preparation.

"First," said Robert in a definite British accent, "we must check to make sure our instruments are clean and free of any experiment pollutants which would taint our process."

"True, true, aye, tis true," said Tim in his best *Muppet Christmas Carol* movie accent.

"Clean cloth," called out Robert.

"Cloth clean," answered Tim, retrieving one from a drawer.

Robert eyed the cloth for contaminants, and, seeing none, he carefully laid it out on the bench.

When this was done, both boys lifted and examined the test tubes, tongs, and beakers next to the bench's sink which was fitted with a tall, chrome-plated faucet.

"Ready," said Robert. Reaching down, he retrieved an opaque plastic bag from his backpack. He opened it and pulled out a small container. After removing its lid, he dumped its light-yellow contents into a large, glass scientific flask.

"Light the Bunsen burner," directed Robert.

Tim lit the Bunsen burner and, using tongs, put the flask above the burner on a rack.

"We shall now turn this semi-solid material into its liquid state," Robert announced.

When the substance was fully melted, Robert removed the flask from the burner and added more compounds, stirring them in one by one. He carefully eyed the measurement, nodded, and said, "Tim, we may now proceed. The critical measurement is established."

"Yes," Tim said, "Critical measurement, set."

"Stirring rod," Robert said to Tim.

"Stirring rod," Tim replied, handing him a narrow, pencil-shaped, transparent glass rod.

Robert carefully began stirring the compound in the flask. "At this point," he announced to the class in formal British accent, "we must be most careful. All the components must be thoroughly mixed, or the experiment will fail."

"Next ingredient," said Robert. "One ovoid."

"One complete ovoid?" said Tim. "Do you not think we should a-void it?"

"Ha, ha," said Robert. "Scientific humor. This is a critical ingredient. Without it, the experiment would demise."

"I see," said Tim. "We must have none such demised experiments on our account."

Robert and Tim felt the eyes of the professor and fellow classmates on them. The canned, overhead lights added even more perspiration to their already sweaty foreheads.

The professor jotted down some notes on his grading sheet.

Robert carefully added the ovoid, minus its clear liquid part, into the flask. He then added several more compounds, stirring them together thoroughly.

"And now for the tricky part. Ingredient number five can be quite reactive. Students of the audience, you would be wise to guard your faces with your backpacks."

"Precisely," said Tim.

"And now, once again for the heat," said Robert, moving the beaker back to above the burner. "Bunsen burner deployed and lit."

"Burner lit," said Tim.

As their mixture heated up, it began to bubble.

"Wow," said a student on the front row. "Look at that endothermic reaction. The color has changed from a mild to a very dark brown."

"Yes, very endothermic-like," Tim replied.

"Definitely not exothermic," said Robert. "That would not be proper for our experiment."

The boys turned off the gas to the Bunsen burner.

"And now for the final test," said Robert. After letting the compound cool for a moment, he probed at it with the stirring rod. "It appears to be ready. We must do one last test to prove it has been properly and completely re-created, that we have matched a previous experiment."

Robert and Tim both got out silver, spoon-like tools. Robert reached his down into the flask and took out a small scoop. Tim followed his example.

"As you can see," said Robert, holding up the dark brown material for all to view. "The materials have been changed into a semi-porous, somewhat rigid substance. Smell has changed. Consistency has changed. It has been chemically changed and cannot be returned back to its original elements."

"What do you think, Robert?" said Tim. "Should we do the final, absolute test?"

"Yes, the primary, ultimate sacrifice; we shall...we must...we will *taste* it for science," Robert replied.

"Oh, no way," said one of the students from the front row. "No, don't do it. It could be un-organic or something."

"Don't do it," said another student, this time in the second row.

"Wow, you're so brave," a student called out from the back of the classroom. "And all for science."

"Yes," Tim replied as he and Robert, in perfect synchronization, took their spoon-like tools and lifted them to their mouths.

"Wait a minute," the professor said, "I can't let you

students do this. It's too dangerous!"

But it was too late. Tim and Robert—eyes closed and wincing—each took a bite.

Everybody watched and gasped in fearful suspense.

"They might die," said a student. "Somebody dial 9-1-1."

Two students fainted, three wanted the Wright cousins' autographs, and the rest of the class shielded their eyes from possible radiation. Robert and Tim stepped to the far end of the bench, opposite from the teacher.

Realizing he was almost out of time, the teacher stood and asked for calm. He reminded the students that their major project was due the next week. The end-of-class bell rang, and the students filed out of the classroom. Robert and Tim quickly cleaned up their tools and left.

"Robert," said Tim, once they were out of the classroom, "that was a good plan. Those were the best *Minute-and-a-half Brownies* I've ever eaten. What do you say we go get some more lunch?"

CHAPTER 3

Jobs

Their royal highnesses, the Princesses Sarina, Katrina, and Maria Straunsee had evacuated from their country of Gütenberg to the United States on the same plane as the Wright cousins. War was imminent in Gütenberg and their father, King Alexander Straunsee, had sent his daughters to America to be clear of the fighting. Their friends, Mr. and Mrs. Olsen, had gone with them as their chaperones.

The Straunsees and their chaperones were living in a rented home with a 24-hour security guard assigned to watch it. It was in a safe neighborhood just a few miles away from the Wright cousins' homes. The Straunsee girls were grateful to be in America. They were enjoying their anonymity—being able to travel around town without anybody really noticing them—but all that was about to change.

Unable to escape the call of school, the Straunsee girls were also playing catch-up like the Wright cousins, the only difference being that the princesses were doing it through online courses. This was a common occurrence for the princesses because they had rarely been able to attend regular school. In fact, they were eager to see what an American school was like.

As a fun surprise, Jonathan had invited his special friend,

17-year-old Princess Sarina Straunsee, to attend one day of classes with him. The Olsen's had some important business to transact, so they gave permission for all three of the girls to go. Sarina would attend with Jonathan, Katrina would attend with Robert, Lindy, and Kimberly in their Junior classes, and 13-year-old Maria—despite Tim's complaints that she had cooties—would attend with Tim.

When they arrived at school, it turned out to be "Job Day," the day when the students would announce the job they would like to possibly do as a profession. Much to Tim's dismay, jobs like *Professional Goof Off*, *Cartoon Watcher*, and *Popcorn Eater* were not on the list.

The day began well enough. Eighteen-year-old Jonathan helped the Straunsees get permission slips from an office secretary. The bell rang and the teenagers rushed to class.

Home rooms were a bit scrambled as the students tried to put the last-minute touches on their "Job Reports." In their job report assignments, the students were to tell their classmates about the jobs of their dreams. The twist, though, was that they had to pick a job within that class's field of study. For their math class, they had to choose a profession that used math, science, a job within the sciences, and so forth. It meant not one report but a report for *each* class period. The one good thing—in Tim's eyes, at least—was that their report could be no longer than 3 minutes each.

For P.E., Tim chose "Operating a Professional Baseball Training School." Robert chose making solar-powered skateboards, and Lindy, using her photographic memory, chose "Becoming a Professional Athlete Statistician."

In Tim's social studies class, each of the students took turns standing in the front of the class and giving their report. On the board behind them was a list of many professions involving history skills.

Miss Reynaldo, Tim's teacher, called a student named Chad to the front of the class to give his report.

Chad walked up to the front of the class and introduced himself. "My name is Chad. I am a diesel mechanic. I fix cars and trucks and large tractors. My responsibilities—." Chad glanced down at his note card, "are to diag...diagnose problems, acquire the proper parts, and repair the...the equipment."

The teacher whispered to Chad, "This is Social Studies."

"Oh," said Chad, his face turning red, "I mean—." Chad reached into his back pocket and pulled out several three-by-five cards. "For social studies, I would want to be a painter."

"That's Art," said Miss Reynaldo. "Try again."

Chad pulled out another card. "A biologist? Social studies teacher?"

"*Bingo,*" smiled Miss Reynaldo.

Tim was next.

"My name is Tim Wright. I want to be an astronaut and a pilot so that I can travel around and do social studies of all kinds of places. I have already flown a spaceplane. My duties will be to fly airplanes and spaceships to visit with different people around the world and the galaxy."

When Tim was done, the teacher invited guest Maria to stand before the class and tell her job.

"My name is Maria Alexa Sutherlee Ruthina Straunsee. I am Tim's friend. I already have a social studies job. *I am a princess.*"

Several students in the class giggled.

"Class!" said the teacher sweetly. "Be *nice* or you will all get *detention.* Okay, go ahead, Maria, and what *would* your job duties be as a princess?"

"My responsibilities as a princess are to help host royal receptions, entertain royal guests, spread good will through friendship and kindness, and help my father, the king."

"Like Cinderella or Sleeping Beauty or Jasmine?" taunted one of the girls from the back of the room.

"Oh no, like me," said Maria. "That is what I do. I am a princess."

"Of course," said the teacher patronizingly, "*every* girl is a princess."

Laughter broke out in the class and the teacher tried to settle the students down again. "Class, class, please," said Miss Reynaldo. "Maria, you will need to choose another profession. You can't just apply to be a princess."

"I don't have to apply," said Maria, drawing herself up to her full height. "I was born a princess and I will stay a princess." She thought for a moment. "If you need my credentials, just ask my twin brother, Timothy Wright."

All eyes turned to Tim. Blushing beet red, he picked up a paper from his desk, held it in front of his face, and slid down low in his desk seat.

"Timothy Wright?" said Miss Reynaldo, "I didn't know you were of royal lineage. Have you been holding out on us?"

Tim could feel the stares of the classroom students burning a hole in the paper he was covering his face with. Sweat was forming on his forehead.

"Tim, tell them," said Maria. "Tell them who you are."

Tim slowly lowered the paper from his face. The eyes of the whole classroom were on him. He glanced at Maria and then at the teacher and said, "Maria is a family friend...of our family. She is thirteen...and I am...fourteen. We were born a few minutes apart because our birthdays aren't on the same day. Maria lives...in a castle...because she is a...princess."

"Thank you, Timothy," said Miss Reynaldo. "I think it would be best—rather than disrupt our class anymore—for you two to take this matter up with the principal."

"The principal?" whispered Tim's friend, Gabe, from the seat behind him. "You're really in trouble now!"

"Maria *is* a princess," said Tim, growing desperate and trying to persuade the teacher to not send them to the office.

"Ooo," teased a boy from the back of the class, "Tim's got a sweet princess."

"I do not," said Tim. "She is a princess all by herself."

"Class," said Miss Reynaldo. "Everyone please be quiet! Now Timothy, do take your friend to the principal's office."

"She *is* a princess. I rescued her from a castle dungeon and we stopped the bad guy lady from escaping by throwing snowballs at her. Princess Maria has 24 hour-a-day cartoons on her phone. She came with us to America because her country is being attacked by Colonel Slagg's country."

Miss Reynaldo was almost buying his story but then Lyle spoke up and said, "Cool video game, Tim, when can I play?"

"Video game? Nice try, Timothy," said Miss Reynaldo. "Please go to the office and explain the matter to the principal. I'll not have my class disrupted."

Frustrated and embarrassed, Tim started gathering up his books. He glanced at Maria. She had tears forming in her eyes. He looked quickly around the class and called out loudly, "*She is so a princess, you'll see!*"

Tim grabbed Maria's wrist and quickly led her out of the classroom.

The principal wasn't in her office, so Tim and Maria were ushered in to meet with the vice principal.

"Timothy Wright, what is it this time?" asked Vice Principal Greenton. Mr. Greenton glanced at Maria and then said, "In a few short words—both of you—what happened? And please be quick about it; I've got a lot of paperwork to do."

"This is Maria," began Tim. "Miss Reynaldo didn't believe Maria here is a real princess."

"Are you a real princess?" asked Mr. Greenton.

"Yes," said Maria, nodding.

Mr. Greenton shook his head and pushed an intercom button. "Sylvia, please tell Dan that I'm going to be tied up for a while. I've got to get to the bottom of this."

Mr. Greenton sat back in his chair, folded his arms, and said seriously, "Okay, Timothy Wright and Maria, tell me about it. How did you disrupt Miss Renaldo's class today?"

"Well," Tim said matter-of-factly, "Maria's dad is the King of Gütenberg...and Maria says I'm her twin brother, and her father is glad that I rescued her from the dungeon...there weren't really any dragons in there that I saw...and we had to stop the bad guys—."

"Wow," said Mr. Greenton, "slow down a little. First off, what is Gütenberg, and if you were her twin brother, wouldn't that make you a prince, Timothy Wright?"

Mr. Greenton was still trying to make sense of the matter when the school bell rang. He finally just threw his hands up in the air and said, "Whatever you're doing, please don't. I'm counting on you, Maria and Tim, to be more respectful in class and help your teacher to be able to teach her material each day. Do you understand me?"

"Yes," mumbled Tim and Maria at the same time.

The school bell rang again and Mr. Greenton ushered Tim and Maria out of his office to the main entry. "Thank you for your cooperation," said Mr. Greenton.

After Tim and Maria were gone, Clarissa, a school financial secretary, asked, "What was Tim in for this time?"

"Something about Gütenberg royalty and dungeons." replied Mr. Greenton. "It must be some kind of new live action video game or something. Boy, the kids today buy into the craziest things."

"You *do* know there is a real kingdom named Gütenberg, don't you?" said Clarissa. "My husband and I saw it on the news this morning. Something about a possible war."

"A kingdom, huh? Tim and Maria must have seen it, too," Mr. Greenton said. "It's probably what gave them the idea about this whole prince and princess stuff. I think I'll pull up their phone numbers so I can have a chat with their parents. We'll have no more of this royal tomfoolery around here."

CHAPTER 4

Changing Worlds

Unbeknownst to the Wright cousins and the Straunsee girls, an article was written that afternoon for the high school news. It went online and spread from there. Titled "Princesses Make Surprise Visit to Local High School," it included photos of Sarina and Katrina Straunsee chatting with Kimberly and other students in a classroom. By 3 o'clock, it had gone viral.

Meanwhile, Jonathan and Sarina had driven over to the local community college to pick up classwork for Tim and Robert.

"Should I bring my sword?" asked Sarina. Sarina's father, King Straunsee, had taught her to be an excellent sword fighter as part of her self-defense training.

"I don't think you'll need it here at the college campus," Jonathan replied with a smile.

The sidewalks were filled with students as Sarina and Jonathan headed for the professor's office. They stopped at an information booth to get directions.

"Hi," said Jonathan, "we're looking for the Gifford building."

"Sure," said the young woman. She retrieved a map to show Jonathan and Sarina the way and drew a circle around the building, plotting the path. She handed the map to

Jonathan, glanced at Sarina, and said, "Hey, aren't you one of those princesses from Gütenberg? I saw your picture on the internet today."

"What do you mean?" asked Sarina.

"Your picture at the high school went viral," said the girl. "Boy, I wish I could do something like that. I'm lucky to even get ten people to look at my social media posts."

A young man standing nearby overheard the conversation, secretly took a picture of Sarina, sent it to his buddy elsewhere on campus, and made a quick phone call.

"Viral?" Sarina whispered to Jonathan with concern, "we didn't really need that."

Jonathan quickly thanked the girl for the map and he and Sarina set off.

As Jonathan and Sarina followed the map, they were led to a courtyard lined with booths and the crowd of students grew even more dense. They read a banner which said, "*Taste of the World* Food Fair." Hundreds of students were eagerly tasting samples of different foods from around the world.

Smelling the sweet aroma of fried scones, Jonathan and Sarina stopped so they could get a free sample.

They were each given a hot scone, topped with melted honey and butter, on a paper napkin.

"This is totally delicious," said Sarina after she had taken a bite.

"I know, right?" Jonathan said. "I've always liked these things."

After finishing their scones, Jonathan and Sarina continued toward the Gifford building. There, they picked up the papers for Robert and Tim and started back to their car. They passed a building under construction. The sidewalk in front of it was blocked off with barricade handrails which led them onto a well-travelled lawn. They passed by two large dumpsters. The crowd grew thick again. Jonathan was now a few feet ahead of Sarina as they squeezed through the thronging students. Two young men pushed between Sarina and Jonathan, separating them even more.

Sarina heard someone call out for help. She stopped to see who it was. She heard the high-pitched, female voice call again. "Help me!"

Sarina turned to look for Jonathan but couldn't see him in the crowd.

"Help me!" the voice called again urgently. Nobody else seemed to hear it.

Concerned, Sarina slipped past the barricade rail and into the construction zone. Moving towards the sound, she soon found herself between two tall buildings about twenty-five feet apart. It was like an alleyway and contained stacks of lumber and other construction materials.

"Help me!" called out the desperate voice again.

Following the voice, Sarina rounded a corner and had gone about ten feet when three rough-looking, college-aged young men stepped out from the shadows in front of her. They reeked of trouble.

"Help me!" called out the obvious leader, the guy in the middle, in a mocking voice. "I've never been kissed by a *real* princess before. Hey, babe, how about a kiss?"

Sarina quickly glanced behind her. Two more creeps had slithered out of the shadows to cut her off.

"No thank you," said Sarina, her defenses at full alert. "You're not my type."

"It wasn't a question," said the leader, stepping closer to the princess. "*Nobody* says *no* to me."

Sarina glanced around, looking for a way out. To her right,

a few feet away, Sarina spied a wooden pole. It was about 1½ inches in diameter, about 6 feet long, and was leaning against a crate.

With an explosion of motion, Sarina bolted sideways and grabbed the oakwood pole, gripping it with two hands like a fighting staff. Then, taking a deep breath, she planted her feet and adjusted her stance to face the five men now surrounding her.

"Ooo, a goody-goody girl," said the gang leader sarcastically. "You want to play rough, huh?"

"That's telling her, Creepo," said one of the gang members.

"I'm not playing," Sarina warned. "And if you were smart, you'd get out of my way."

"Not on your life, princess," Creepo replied. "My government has a big bounty on your royal head. With the reward from capturing you and your sisters, we'll be rich."

The gang members closed in threateningly around Sarina.

"I'm warning you," Sarina said, waving her pole offensively to keep them at a distance. She knew that if one of them got hold of her staff it would be all over. There was no way she could alone beat their upper body strength. To win this fight, Sarina had to play to *her* strengths; she needed to be swift and agile.

"This is gonna be fun," said the gang leader.

"Not for you, you sleazy lowlife," returned Sarina.

One of the gang members stepped forward. In a flash, Sarina used the pole to **WHACK** him on the head. He went crashing to the ground, knocked out cold. The gang was surprised.

Sarina quickly stepped back to her defensive position. "Now back off!" she ordered.

"No way," said the gang leader, taking a threatening step

toward Sarina. The princess swung the right end of the oak staff and hit him forcefully in the chest, knocking him back.

Angrily gripping his chest in pain, he gasped and growled, "You'll pay for that, *missy!*"

Creepo started for her again. Sarina lunged forward and slammed him in the stomach and ribs, doubling him over in pain.

The gang members to the left of Sarina rushed forward. She spun around, hitting the first one in the ribs and sending him reeling. The second, she whacked in the chest and jaw, knocking him to the ground. Sarina hit the third gang member hard on his knees, then on the side of the head, pushing him away.

"Grab the pole!" Creepo cried out angrily. He and two others lunged for Sarina. Sarina caught the guy on the left with a solid slam to his sternum and a whack on his face. He grabbed his nose and chest and staggered backwards. In a whirlwind of motion, Sarina threw all of her weight into the staff, hitting Creepo squarely in the jaw and sending him crashing backwards against a large wooden crate.

Sarina spun around and slammed the last standing gang member in the chest and chin. He crumpled to the ground, unconscious.

Ready to deal out more, Sarina defiantly glared at the five bruised, battered, and bloody-nosed attackers lying around her on the ground. **"You sleazy lowlifes!"** she shouted at them, **"I AM A GOOD GIRL. *DON'T YOU EVER MESS WITH ME AGAIN!"***

Sarina backed up two steps to get clear and then dashed back the way she had come. Reaching the courtyard, she vaulted the barricade and rammed into the throng of students, looking for Jonathan.

"Sarina," a voice called out, "over here!"

Sarina turned to see Jonathan running and pushing through the crowd toward her. She pushed through the crowd to meet him.

"Sarina, where have you been?" said Jonathan, reaching her. "I've been looking all over for you."

"Five guys attacked me...in that alleyway over there," she replied between breaths. "I was able to fight them off with this pole."

"Are you okay?" said Jonathan worriedly.

"Yes," Sarina replied shakily, "I'm crazy full of adrenaline right now, but I'm okay. Call the police. I can't find my phone. And Jonathan, those sleazy lowlifes knew I was a princess. They said there was a big bounty on my head."

"Bounty?" Jonathan said. "Sarina, this is bad. Let's get you out of here!"

Jonathan took her hand and said, "You hold onto my hand tightly, okay? We'll stick with the buddy system."

"Yes," said Sarina with a trembling smile, "no matter what, I won't let go, Jonathan Wright. Don't you let go of me, either."

"That's for sure," Jonathan replied, "let's get to our car."

Like a football lineman, Jonathan, with Sarina holding onto his hand behind him, plowed his way through the crowd. "Sarina," he called back, "we'll call the others once we're on the road. Boy, am I *glad* your father taught you how to defend yourself!"

"Me, too," said Sarina.

When they reached their car, Sarina handed the oak pole to Jonathan. Jonathan opened the front passenger door for her and she slid into the front seat. Sarina positioned her favorite sword beside her seat as Jonathan closed the door.

With Sarina safe in the car, Jonathan set the pole down in front of their car, got into the driver's seat, and handed his phone to Sarina. Sarina quickly called the Olsens to let them know about the attack and so they could report it to the police in the proper manner. Sarina then phoned her twin sister, Katrina.

Jonathan and Sarina travelled directly to the house where Sarina and her sisters were staying with their chaperones. Out front, there was an unmarked car with a guard sitting in it. A shiny new, fourteen-passenger van was parked in the driveway; its back doors were open, facing the garage. Jonathan noted it had bulletproof glass.

Katrina ran out of the house to meet Sarina. "I'm so grateful you're all right!" Katrina said, hugging her. "You'll have to hurry; we're being moved to a more secure safehouse somewhere. Father says our country's intelligence has picked up intel about groups making plans to kidnap us."

The three of them walked back into the house where they met Robert, Kimberly, Lindy, Tim, and Maria in the living room. They talked momentarily, thankful for Sarina's escape, and then set back to work helping the princesses pack.

Jonathan helped Sarina load her gear, too. Just as they were finishing packing, several security cars pulled up and parked on the street. After quick good-byes, Sarina, Katrina, Maria, and the Olsens climbed into the reinforced van and were whisked away to an undisclosed destination.

The Wright cousins climbed back into their family minivan. Their world was suddenly upside-down. Sarina had been attacked in the cousins' hometown!

"It's my fault," said Jonathan as he drove. "I should never have invited Sarina to see our high school."

"How could we know this would happen?" asked Kimberly.

"Besides, who would expect that silly high school *Job Day* story would go viral?"

"Yeah, who would have thought?" said Tim, "I mean, the vice principal wouldn't even believe me in his office when I told him Maria was a real princess."

Tim suddenly clapped his hand over his mouth.

"Since when were you in the principal's office?" asked Kimberly suspiciously.

"We...um...were just visiting...at Miss Reynaldo's request," Tim replied, quickly changing the subject. "Jonathan, I can't believe what happened to you and Sarina at the college."

"I'm just grateful Sarina knows how to defend herself and could beat the tar out of them," said Jonathan.

"Yes, thank goodness," said Lindy. "Maybe we should all take a self-defense class."

"This is so bad," said Jonathan, "what are we going to do? I was really looking forward to being able to play host to Sarina and her sisters around here. You know, show them some of our old stomping grounds, introduce them to great Aunt Opal, take them for a flight in our Grumman Duck seaplane, maybe even get to show them the Spanish galleon treasure ship. Now it's all been wrecked because that crazy high school story went viral."

"So, Tim," Kimberly said, returning to the subject, "what was that about you and Maria being at the vice principal's office?"

CHAPTER 5

pH Balance

That afternoon, Robert and Tim got back to work on their "Leuco Dye" chemistry experiment at Tim's house.

"We'll have to keep this a trade secret," said Robert as he glanced at a paint ingredients reference manual.

"I don't want to trade it," said Tim. "We've got to keep it."

"It's just a term. A 'trade secret' is where you don't let anybody know about how to make it."

"Oh," said Tim, "but you and I don't have to keep it secret from each other, do we?"

"Only from everybody else," said Robert.

"Okay," Tim said with a relieved smile, "that sounds better. So, how do we make it?"

"Good question," Robert replied. "But I think I might have an idea."

Robert took out a piece of paper and started writing on it with a pencil. Tim watched as Robert began writing different formulas, erasing part of them here and there, and often combining them. The one page turned into many.

Tim knew that when Robert got into his "scientific mode," it could be a while before he emerged from his formulas. Tim used the time to find and gather his favorite toy trucks and cars. By the time Robert looked up and put his mechanical pencil behind his right ear, Tim had twenty-one cars ready for painting.

"Okay," said Robert finally, "I think I've got it. We're going to have two different experiments. The first one, Plan A, will be the leuco dye color-changing paint on your toy cars. Plan B, the emergency back-up plan, is the one I've been working on at my house. I'll tell you about it later."

From the Wright cousins' experience, Robert had grown to appreciate back-up plans because their original plans sometimes failed.

"Good, Tim," said Robert, "you've got the cars. The first thing we'll have to do is get them super clean. We can wash them with dish soap and water so they can be drying while we get our ingredients together for making the paint."

Robert headed to his house a few blocks away while Tim got the cleaning items together. In the kitchen, Tim got a large plastic bowl, dish soap, and hand towel. By the time Robert got back with a big box full of supplies, Tim was scrubbing away on the cars and setting them out to dry on a towel on the bathroom sink countertop.

"Hey, you're pretty good at that," said Robert.

"Yeah," Tim said, "Kimberly has been making me do the dishes a lot more. She used to do them all the time but she's on this 'Tim, you need to learn more basic life skills' thing. Besides, I owe her five dollars for accidentally vacuuming up one of her sandals."

"Using that toothbrush to scrub the cars and trucks, especially those muddy ones, was genius," said Robert.

"Yeah, it really reaches into all the hard places to clean. I couldn't find my toothbrush, so I had to use Kimberly's. You don't think she'll mind, do you?" Tim replied. "She did say she really wanted to help me succeed in our chemistry class."

"What was that?" called out Kimberly from the living room.

"Nothing," Tim replied, "we're just cleaning up some of my old toys."

"Well, hurry please," Kimberly said. "I need to shower after I finish cleaning and dusting the dining room and living room. You've got about twenty minutes. Mom and I are going shopping. Oh, and don't get the bathroom dirty, I just cleaned it. You guys can take out the trash when you're done."

"Okay," said Tim and Robert at the same time.

Turning on the bathroom fan, Robert donned his safety goggles and went to work while Tim tried to get the mud and grit out of Kimberly's toothbrush at the sink.

"We were doing it all wrong before," Robert explained as he measured and poured chemicals. "We were trying to use nitrogen and glycerin. That's why we kept having all those explosions. And the saltpeter didn't work, either; it kept turning into gunpowder. Leuco paints are a whole different story. It's all about controlling the hydrogen potential."

"Okay, whatever you say," nodded Tim. "Let's just hurry and get it done. I've got to get some more cartoons drawn up for my high school fine art class."

Twenty-three minutes later, Robert and Tim had their test products assembled. There was more quantity than they had expected so they had to come up with larger containers.

Tim spied two empty plastic bottles in the bathroom trash can. He retrieved them and said, "There, now the trash is empty."

Robert and Tim quickly rinsed them out and poured their two Plan A, "Leuco dye," products into them for use later.

Plan A was now ready for testing. Robert wanted to hurry and complete his notes for the experiment, so he set the bottles on the countertop next to the Plan B shampoo bottles he had brought from home. Tim retrieved a permanent marker, and they labeled the bottles A, B, C, and D. A and B were the leuco paints, C and D were Plan B.

Robert had stumbled upon Plan B over at Tim's house several days before. He had overheard his twin sister, Lindy, and cousin Kimberly, complaining about their hair having "split ends."

"Why doesn't somebody come up with a *real* treatment that will fix split ends," said Kimberly. "I mean, if we can orbit the earth and fly to the moon, why can't we stop our hair from looking like a frayed carpet?"

"If anybody can do it," Lindy said, "Robert can. I'll talk to him about it."

Robert did investigate why split ends occur and what might be done to take care of them. He found that split ends can happen naturally to everyone and need to be cut off if they get really bad.

He discovered three potential causes: heat, chemicals, and combing.

To stop heat from causing split ends, blow dryers can be used on a cooler setting or kept farther away from the hair.

Harsh chemicals used for bleaching, coloring, perming and hair relaxing can also cause split ends. Spreading out these kinds of treatments can reduce the stress on the hair.

Combing with a wide-toothed comb helps the comb glide through the hair easier and not kink it. Over-combing can cause split ends, too.

Robert also discovered that moisturizers could help hair not get split ends.

Robert didn't really get into all the hair-coloring stuff, so he focused on the "moisturizing" part. He found several recommended moisturizers listed, including aloe vera, coconut oil, bananas, and even honey.

"Wow," Robert said to Tim, "can you imagine Winnie-the-Pooh stuck in a tall, old oak tree with honey all over him. I just don't see how honey would help. It seems like it would just stick your hair together and make a big mess."

"We could try it on your hair to see if it works," said Tim.

"Actually," Robert replied, "I was thinking we could try it on *your* hair."

Seeing a "mad scientist" gleam in Robert's eye, Tim quickly covered his hair with a baseball cap.

For Plan B, Robert and Tim rounded up some old fur skins to test their concoctions on. They located a tanned, rabbit skin, a raccoon tail on Robert's old Davy Crockett raccoon skin hat, and a cowhide satchel that still had the hair on it. It had to be *real* hair, though, so the fake-fur trimmed hood on Kimberly's parka coat was safe from their experiments.

Kimberly was just finishing her dusting. The boys quickly rounded up their supplies, put them in the box, wiped down the countertop, and set Kimberly's toothbrush back in its rack. In their haste, the boys forgot the paints and moisturizers. There were now four black shampoo bottles resting against the splashboard on the countertop nearest the shower. Except for their letter labels, they looked exactly alike.

Robert and Tim headed for Tim's room to write up their experiment report. By the time they realized they had left their experiment bottles in the bathroom, Kimberly and her mom were already at the store. Robert and Tim retrieved the bottles and headed back to Tim's room to paint the toy cars.

They tried dipping a car but found it too messy. They tried different sizes of paint brushes. The paint was too thick, then it was too thin. After masking the wheels and windshields with tape, they tried using a water spray bottle. It worked okay for a short time but then it clogged. In the end, they wound up using small, model type paintbrushes. Keeping copious notes, they recorded what they did with each car.

After the cars were all painted with their basecoat and dried, the boys next painted on the second layer of paint. The second layer was supposed to be colored when cold and then turn clear—revealing the base coat color—when warmed.

Again, they let the cars dry. Three of the cars they dried with a hair dryer to speed up the process. It worked on two of the cars but on the third one, Tim got it too hot, and it burned the paint and melted the cab windows.

"I guess this is the junkyard car," said Tim, setting the car aside.

"We'd better keep it, Timbo, so we can show what too much heat can do," Robert said. "It's still part of the experiment."

The tops of the leuco dye paint bottles needed to be cleaned, so they took them back to the bathroom to wash them off and left them there to dry.

Robert and Tim were taking a break in the backyard, playing catch with a baseball, when Kimberly and her mom got home. Tim tossed the ball back to Robert and then went in to see what kind of food goodies his mom had bought.

"Can you please help me bring in the rest of the groceries, honey?" Tim's mom asked.

"Sure," said Tim, noting his sister was trying to rinse something out of her hair at the kitchen sink, "what's wrong with Kimberly?"

"A little girl in a shopping cart dropped a toy," his mom replied. "When Kimberly went to pick it up for her, the girl dumped some apple-berry juice on Kimberly's hair. It's been itching her like crazy."

"I'm going to have to take another shower," Kimberly announced, wringing out her hair over the sink and heading for her room to get her robe and towel. When she was done showering, she dried her hair and started combing it out. Her hair still looked a little reddish so she shampooed her hair again to get the berry juice out. "Great," she mumbled in frustration, "we've got school pictures in two days, and I've got berry juice stain in my hair."

Kimberly shampooed her hair two more times to get it clean.

"Something must be wrong with the lighting in the dining room tonight," said Dad. "Kimberly's hair is looking kind of purple."

"Oh, it's just the berry juice that got spilled on her this afternoon," said Mom.

Rather than embarrass Kimberly anymore, the subject was dropped.

The next afternoon, after school, Robert came back over to Tim's house so they could work more on their projects. Lindy went with him to visit with Kimberly. Kimberly met them at the door and invited them in.

"Kimberly, did you touch up your hair or something?" asked Lindy jokingly.

"Lindy, you know I've never messed with my hair color. I like my natural look. No, a little kid dumped some berry juice on my head at the grocery store," Kimberly replied. "It's been really hard to get it out."

"Well, don't worry, I'm sure it's not permanent," said Lindy.

Robert slipped on past the girls and went to find Tim. Tim was in the backyard lining up his toy trucks.

"Tim, does Kimberly's hair look any different to you?"

asked Robert. "It seems darker."

"Oh, you mean the juice stuff?" said Tim.

"No, more than that. Maybe she's just getting older," Robert said, answering his own question. "Your hair does get darker as you get older."

"But what about when it turns white?" Tim replied. "In the state where my friend, Travis Snowbird, lives, the first thing the people do when they move there is bleach their hair. I don't know why everybody wants to be blonde anyways, we have just as much fun as them."

"Thank you, Tim-with-the-honey-blond-hair," said Kimberly from the house backdoor, standing in the warm sunlight. "What are you guys up to today?"

"Oh, just fine-tuning our chemistry projects," Robert replied. He did a double-take. "Kimberly, since when did you have red hair?"

"What are you talking about?" said Kimberly, feeling her long, normally blonde hair. She took some of her hair in her hand and gasped. Her hair was turning bright red and the more she looked at it, the redder it became. "What's happening?!" she called out in panic.

CHAPTER 6

Bad Hair Day

"No! No! No! No! No!" said Kimberly. "What's going on with my hair? This can't be happening!"

"What was in that juice?" said Tim.

"I don't think it was the juice," Lindy said from behind Kimberly. "This is something major."

"But your hair can't just start turning colors, can it?" said Kimberly.

"Maybe it's some kind of disease," said Tim.

"Thanks, Tim," said Kimberly, grabbing some of her long hair and looking it over. It seemed to be turning redder by the second. "Lindy, what's going on? My hair has never done this before!"

"I told you that you were eating too many carrots and tomatoes," said Tim. "Now look what you've done."

"Carrots, tomatoes, and a little kid's juice box wouldn't do this," said Lindy. "Kimberly, did you change shampoos or something?"

"No," Kimberly replied. "I just used my regular stuff in the bathroom. Tim, you didn't put anything in my shampoo, did you?"

"Of course not," Tim replied.

"Kimberly," said Robert, rubbing his chin, "did you

accidentally use some of our experimental paint?"

"I don't think so," said Kimberly, "the shampoo in the shower was empty, so I got some of the new stuff off the sink counter."

"Oh no!" said Robert.

"Oh no!" said Tim.

"Oh no!" said Kimberly.

"Wow, it worked better on your hair than on my trucks," said Tim.

"It does give you a whole new look," said Lindy, encouragingly.

"Yes," said Robert, "it's like a *secret agent* Wright disguise."

"But I like my real hair color," groaned Kimberly, "what can I do?"

"Well," said Tim, "you could come to our chemistry class to show them how good it works."

"I don't want to be Exhibit A," said Kimberly, "I want my hair back. This is crazy."

Lindy was studying Kimberly's hair. It was red clear down to the roots.

"You could try getting regular shampoo and see if it will come out after a wash or two," said Lindy. "I'd be happy to help you at the sink."

Kimberly retrieved a brand-new bottle of shampoo from their storage room and the girls went to work. But it didn't do any good.

It wasn't so obvious at first, but over the next several hours, Kimberly's hair almost seemed to change colors according to temperature and, perhaps, even her mood. When her hair was cold, it looked more bluish. When Kimberly got excited about something, more yellow or orange. When she was upset, it seemed to turn more red.

Tim told Robert that sometimes it was more fun to watch Kimberly's hair change colors than it was to watch cartoons, and for Tim, that's saying something.

"I'll tell you a secret," Tim said, "if you pay attention to Kimberly's hair, she's definitely more fun to be around when her hair is more bluish. You know her personality; when her hair is bright red, *dive for cover!*"

The next afternoon, Kimberly was sitting in the sun under the grape arbor. When she went to move, Tim chuckled because her hair had a crisscross, lattice-work pattern on it. It was bright red where it had been in the sun and bluer where it had been in the shade.

Kimberly tried wearing a knit beanie hat to high school, but the teachers wouldn't let her keep it on in the classroom. They said it was "rude to wear a hat indoors." So, when Kimberly had to take her hat off in her art painting class, the students all set down their brushes and stared in surprise at her red-tinted hair.

"Wow, *bad* hair, Kim," said one of her friends with a smile and then they all went back to work on their paintings.

One of the main challenges Kimberly ran into with her hair color changing was trying to dress to match or accent her hair. It's one thing if your hair is blonde. Purples and blues often go well with that. But Kimberly was dealing with hair tints of blue, yellow, green, orange—just how does one dress for orange hair?—and red.

Usually, she would try to go with the complimentary colors but with her hair changing color so often, she had to settle on generic blouses with a lot of different colors, and blue jeans.

The next day, school pictures were being taken. Each time Kimberly went out to brush her hair to get ready, her hair changed colors.

"Wait a minute, it's not your turn," said the photographer. "That blonde-haired girl will be right back."

Kimberly brushed her hair more to try to make it blonde. It turned orange instead. She looked in the mirror and saw it; her frustration then turned it red!

Kimberly got some water on her wide-toothed comb and tried that approach. She now had red, yellow, and blue stripes in her hair. Another brush and somehow, she got white polka dots on blue with red and white stripes.

"Hey, that's cool," said the photographer when Kimberly came back in. "I like the patriotic look."

*   *   *

The Straunsee girls' new "safehouse" was part of an old folks, 65+ senior citizen community in a neighboring town. The Wrights got clearance to visit them with one hitch: they had to look like 65-year-olds! Picture Timothy Wright with white hair, a white moustache, blue jeans, and white tennis shoes. Kimberly, of course, had to wear a grey wig because her hair refused to stop changing colors. It gave the Wright cousins an opportunity to work on their disguise talents.

"By crackie," said Robert, leaning over to whisper into Tim's ear, "I haven't felt this old since I was seventeen!"

"But you *are* seventeen," Tim whispered back, leaning on the long wooden cane he was holding.

"Oh, yeah, right," Robert whispered.

"Kind of makes me glad we did all of our adventurin' all those years ago," whispered Tim. "I'm too tired and creakety to do it nowadays. My getup has just done got up and went."

Jonathan, Robert, and Tim had an "old timer's race" from the car to the new safehouse's front door. Canes at the ready,

Jonathan creaked in first, Robert shuffled in second, and Tim teetered in last.

"This is rough," whispered Tim. "I never knew being old was so difficult."

A security guard met the Wright cousins at the front door and ushered them into the living room where Sarina, Katrina, and Maria were waiting. The thick curtains were drawn closed.

"Thank you so much for coming," said Katrina, once they were all seated on couches. Tim sat down on a swivel recliner chair and was already starting to spin around as the friends all talked.

"Father says there are many enemy agents trying to find us," said Katrina. "I hope you don't get mixed up in our mess."

"Yes," said Sarina, "Jonathan, I've been thinking, maybe you and I should act as if we don't, well, you know, *like* each other? That way our enemies would leave you alone."

"Good luck with *that*," Tim chuckled as he spun around and around in the swivel recliner chair, "you guys are thicker than peanut butter."

"The kid does have a good point," said Jonathan with a smile, "I don't think we'd be very convincing."

Sarina, blushing slightly, grinned back, and said, "Yeah, I guess it is kind of obvious, huh? Okay, *next* idea."

"Maybe we could put together some kind of warning system," said Robert. "That way we could communicate and warn each other if something came up."

"Like ham radios?" said Katrina.

CHAPTER 7

Paintball

The cousins were members of a paintball club that went paintballing at a nearby facility once every two months. It gave them a chance to have fun with friends and fellow high school students in the great outdoors for some rough-and-tumble play. And sometimes, it was definitely rough-and-tumble. The cousins always drove their minivan and picked up three friends along the way.

When they arrived at the paintball facility, the cousins and their friends checked in and began to suit up.

Being hit by a paintball can be pretty painful, so the cousins had learned to "layer up" by wearing multiple shirts and pairs of pants. The weather was cool this time so they could dress more warmly and still be comfortable.

Each cousin wore sweatpants underneath their baggier, camouflaged pants, several layers of shirts with long sleeves, and gloves. They also wore olive drab tactical, load-bearing vests. Then came the vital and mandatory helmet, face shield, and ear protection, all over their fabric neck protection. The girls smartly pulled their hair back. Lindy braided her hair and Kimberly put hers in a ponytail to keep it out of the way.

Each of the cousins knew that rule number one was to *always protect their eyes*. Goggles and face shields had to fit firmly and *always* stay in place. Also, paintball marker guns were never to be pointed at anyone before battle, and only then at fifteen feet or more. Paintballs can really carry a wallop!

"I feel like a stuffed starfish," said Tim after getting suited up. "How am I ever going to be able to walk, let alone run?"

"Once we get out on the paintball field and you're getting shot at," Robert replied, patting him on the back, "I don't think you'll have any trouble running."

"Tim, you just keep your face and eye protection in place," said Kimberly as she nervously adjusted her helmet strap. "And keep your head down and don't get shot."

"Yes," Robert added, "and just remember, Timbo, if somebody's shooting at you, they're not your friends."

"Good to remember," said Tim with a nervous grin. Tim had gone paintballing a few times and had gotten some pretty mean bruises. This time, he was suiting up better.

"Okay, we're all set up to go," said Jonathan, just returning from the park's office. "We're Team Green."

Each of the cousins grabbed their paintball gun and headed toward the paintball field. At the paintball park, there were specific areas for "battling" and also no-shoot, or safe, areas. Referees, or Marshals, were in place to rectify any problems or disputes which might happen.

The field included a forested area with horizontal logs, small hills, ravines, and two old barns. Team Green's mission was to capture Team Red's barn and take their flag; Team Red's was to capture Team Green's.

Jonathan was elected to be Green Team captain. As the Wright cousins and their friends, fifteen in all, took their places at the start of the game, they could see Team Red heading over to get into place, too.

"When you hear this bell ring," announced the marshal,

standing near the bell tower, "it means to begin the battle. If you hear the bell at any time during the battle, you are to immediately stop all shooting and point your paintball guns at the ground. May the best team win."

"That means us," yelled the Red Team captain. "You guys are going down!"

"Dream on," Jonathan called back.

Unbeknownst to the Wright cousins, they had been followed to the paintball facility. A car had fallen in line behind them in traffic just as they left town. When the car parked, five college-aged young men got out. They were well familiar with paintball and purposefully joined the opposing team. Their goal was to win not only the competition but also to get some information out of the Wright cousins.

"They'll talk after we loosen them up with a few paintball hits," said the gang's leader, Creepo, with a sneering smile. "It'll be a piece of pie."

"Everybody ready?" called out the marshal.

"Yes," called back the team captains as Creepo's gang filtered into the Red Team.

The bell rang and the teams leapt into action. Green team members cleared out of the main area in a few seconds. They moved in a loose "E" formation, with some members moving along the sides of the field and others moving down the middle, utilizing the shelter of large tree trunks, boulders, and wood and rock walls. Jonathan, Tim, Kimberly, and Robert were following a ravine.

Jonathan quickly led the way as point man. Racing from tree to tree, Robert was second. Tim was third, followed by Kimberly as rearguard. The cousins were spaced about fifteen to twenty feet apart, depending on the shelter available.

Jonathan and Robert had just gotten into position. Tim

was moving up. Robert heard a volley of paintballs smack the tree next to him. He ducked behind a tree and glanced in the direction the shooting was coming from. Seeing someone in the woods, he pulled his gun around, returned fire, and jumped behind a bush. A paintball whizzed by his ears and he hit the dirt.

"Left woods!" Robert called out.

Jonathan pivoted at Robert's shout and fired rapidly in the attacker's direction. The enemy dodged into a thicket and disappeared amongst the trees. Kimberly and Tim moved as a team to intercept them.

Robert and Jonathan crept forward, moving into the cover of the denser trees. Robert saw an enemy taking aim at Tim and pulsed his trigger three times. Two paintballs hit target and splatted on the enemy's left side, effectively kicking him out of the game.

Tim ducked down and ran, hunched over, forward to the next boulder. Kimberly followed him. Eyeing some motion in the forest, Tim caught a Red Team member from the side and pelted him with paintballs.

Two enemies down with the Red Team's flag to go.

Catching Tim's attention, Robert signaled to him about another opponent's position. With the wave of a hand, Tim understood they would attack with a pincer movement, where they would split up and approach him from the side and rear.

Separating, they crawled and sprinted. Tim was just getting into position when several paintballs hit near his feet. Robert was nearly pelted at the same time. In a whirl of motion, Robert ducked, rolled, and hid behind a larger tree trunk. Tim kept running.

Kimberly, carefully hiding behind another tree, saw several opponents in the brush beyond Tim. She cautiously navigated forward into a new position as Tim dodged several paintballs that slammed into a tree next to him.

Keeping his gun hopper—the container on top of the gun which holds the paintballs—level so it would feed right, Tim hurdled a large rock, firing as he jumped, pelting the brush and trees in front of him. Hitting the dirt, he checked the forest; nobody was there!

Tim clambered back to his feet and kept going. Paintballs smacked into the trees around him. Hearing a paintball whistle by, Tim ducked and rolled behind a log just as a volley of paintballs splattered the tree trunk and the ground behind him.

"Need covering fire!" Tim called out.

Kimberly began pumping the trigger on her paintball gun, laying down covering fire for Tim. She was sending paintballs slamming into the bushes and woods beyond Tim.

Keeping his cover behind the big log, Tim army-crawled in the ravine's direction. Just as he was about to stand back up, he saw someone taking aim at Kimberly. He aimed his gun and pelted the opponent with paintballs. The opponent recoiled and fell to the ground.

"I'm out," called out the Red Team member, holding his paintball gun above his head with both hands. It was one of Tim's classmates from high school.

Tim spied Robert across the ravine and waved to him for instructions. Robert pointed to an area in front of Tim and held up two fingers. That meant there were two opponents somewhere in front of Tim.

Tim backed quietly into the brush and made his way toward a small clearing with a large boulder in it. Skirting the area, he tried to see if someone was on the other side of the boulder. There was!

Tim started to raise his gun to aim when a voice from behind him called out, "Don't move. Do you want to surrender or be shot?"

Tim turned around and saw a college age young man, four feet away, aiming at him from behind a tree.

"You got me," said Tim with a mischievous grin. He raised his gun over his head with two hands and said loudly, "Just one problem: I'm not the only one that's out."

The guy behind the tree grunted as he was suddenly hit by several paintballs. He and Tim were soon on their way to the safety zone. They talked about the game and how their teams were doing. The student seemed like a nice enough guy.

"You and your friend did all right on your chemistry demonstration," said the student. "You really faked us out with that brownie experiment."

"Yeah, that was pretty good," said Tim.

"Hey, you're still in high school, too, aren't you?" asked the student.

"Yes," Tim replied.

"So, what was it like to have those princesses visit your school?" asked the student.

"It was okay, I guess," Tim replied. "Princesses are just like everybody else."

"Do you know how we can get in touch with them?" asked the student. "It would be cool to have them visit our campus."

"Dude," Tim said, "princesses have cooties *really* bad. And they even accused *me* of having cooties. And I'm the most cootie-less guy there is."

"Oh," said the student, "I'll have to think about that one."

The bell began ringing, signaling the end of the battle. Green Team had gotten Red Team's flag and were safely back to their base.

The college student, realizing he was running out of time to talk with Tim, said, "So, do you know where the princesses went after the high school."

"Probably to college," said Tim.

"I mean, where did they move to?" asked the student.

"I've got to go," said Tim, and he ran over to his own team.

There was a short break as team members cleaned their gear and got ready for the next battle.

"What did you find out?" asked Creepo.

"I ran out of time," said the student. "I think that kid knows more than he's saying."

"Let's put him out of the game earlier so we can grill him more," said Creepo.

The next battle, Creepo's gang didn't care as much about winning as they did about putting Tim out of the game. Once they located Tim, they surrounded him and fired away. Some of their shots at him were from less than ten feet away, which was totally against the rules.

Tim had mean, red welts from the paintballs on his left arm, back, and stomach. He quickly made his way to the safe zone before they were able to talk with him.

Kimberly was later taken out, too, so she sat by Tim in the safe zone, watching the game. She noted Tim kept holding his arm. "What's wrong?" she asked.

"Those older Red guys hit me hard," Tim replied and showed her some of the welts on his arm and back.

Kimberly got some cold water, soaked a bandanna, and started softly dabbing Tim's wounds. "I'm so sorry," Kimberly said. "Stick with me next battle so we can defend each other better, okay?"

"Sure," said Tim.

The next round, Kimberly and Tim stayed nearer their own

base at the start. Partly to help protect their flag but also to give Tim a chance to recover from his wounds. After several minutes, Tim and Kimberly started to move forward. They moved into the trees on the right side this time. They were soon discovered by several Red Team members who started going after Tim again. Kimberly stayed in the shade; the coolness turned her hair to a bluish color. A Red Team member charged toward Tim. Kimberly nailed him with a triple shot of paintballs.

Tim and Kimberly moved forward to another group of trees, this time the sun was a little warmer. Kimberly didn't notice it but her hair had now turned to blonde. Tim was point man and started to draw fire. Kimberly took out his attacker.

They moved forward again, running across a small meadow to more cover. Kimberly's hair turned orange. They had just reached some new shelter when Tim saw two opponents taking aim at he and Kimberly.

"Look out!" shouted Tim.

CHAPTER 8

Battle

Tim and Kimberly both hit the deck as paintballs whizzed by. The siblings fired back, hitting the two enemies on their chests and face shields.

Crawling to a more secure position behind a log barrier, Tim and Kimberly could hear talking on the other side of the wall.

"Forget about the others," whispered a voice, "we're supposed to get the younger kid that's wearing the black army boots."

Kimberly and Tim signaled back and forth, planning their next attack, and then noiselessly rose to their knees. Tim crawled to the far end of the log wall while Kimberly crept around the other way.

Because of the partial sunlight, Kimberly's hair had now turned green. Through a slit in the wall, Kimberly could see two Red Team members heading in Tim's direction. Kimberly jumped up from her crouched position, fired over the wall, and nailed the two opponents.

Kimberly caught up with Tim and whispered, "Tim, you're sure a good 'bad guy' magnet."

"Thank you, I think," said Tim with a slight grin, "Let's go get some more."

Tim and Kimberly made their way over to a large boulder. The sun was getting warmer. Kimberly's hair was now turning red. The two cousins carefully made their way around to the side of the rock. Four paintballs impacted on the rock beside them. Kimberly and Tim dived and rolled behind a three-foot-tall rock with a bush growing beside it.

"Get to that bush over there," said Tim. "I'll lay down cover fire for you."

"Hit that kid over there by the boulder," called out someone from the trees at the far side of the small meadow.

Several paintballs slammed into the rock in front of Tim and Kimberly. The siblings hunkered down and rapidly crawled to find a safe hiding place.

"There's one by that oak and another by the pine tree to the left," said Tim. He aimed his paintball gun and fired.

There was a short rustle in the brush as Jonathan, Lindy, and Robert charged and took out Kimberly and Tim's attackers.

"Out!" called out two young men, holding their guns over their heads and begrudgingly heading for the safe zone.

"You're clear," called out Jonathan.

"Thanks," said Tim.

Grateful to get out of their exposed position, Kimberly and Tim quickly ran over to meet the other three Wright cousins in the woods.

"We've been looking all over for you guys," said Jonathan. "And by the way, good job. You've been taking out a lot of the enemy."

Kimberly and Tim both grinned. "They've been focusing on getting Tim," said Kimberly. "I've just been picking them off before they get him."

Several paintballs whizzed by their heads. Jonathan, Robert, and Tim were hit multiple times and fell to the ground. Kimberly and Lindy were protected by tree trunks but they, too, dropped to the ground and scooted closer to the trees to hide in the undergrowth and brush.

"Out!" yelled the three boys. Holding their guns above their heads, they marched off the field.

"Rats," said Tim, "and we were just starting to get them."

Lindy and Kimberly lay still in the undergrowth of bushes. They could hear hushed talking nearby.

"Keep focusing on the youngest Wright kid," whispered a voice. "We'll get him to help us, yet."

Lindy and Kimberly glanced at each other in alarm. This time, Kimberly's hair didn't turn red from the sun's warmth; she was downright angry.

Keeping her gun level so it wouldn't jam, Kimberly leapt to her feet. With her hair now blazing bright red, she charged straight for the attackers, tripping the trigger so fast she was firing full auto. "You guys are history!" she called out as she nailed all three of the surprised enemy and put them out of the game. They were petrified.

"Out!" shouted the three young men belatedly. Seeing the fury in Kimberly's eyes, they sprinted off the battlefield before she could even approach them. Kimberly kept her paintball gun aimed at them until they were out of sight.

The game ended soon after that. Both teams began preparing for the next battle, the last war game of the day.

Waiting for the starting bell to ring, the Red Team was talking amongst themselves.

"Who shot you?" asked one member of the Red Team, seeing his buddy covered in paint splatters.

"Some girl with blue hair. How about you?"

"I was shot by a blonde girl," the first replied.

"An orange-haired girl took me out," said a third.

"Not me, I was shot by the redhead," said another, smothered in paint, "and man, was she *scary!*"

"Oh yeah? You want to talk about scary? The one that shot me had green hair, and I mean green," said another team member. "It still gives me the heebie-jeebies."

"What are you guys, a bunch of fraidy-cats?" Creepo asked in a disgusted whisper. "We're going to play another battle and we're going to win this time. No bunch of girls, whatever their hair color is, are going to wreck our plan. We're going to find out where those princesses are and collect on that bounty!"

"But Creepo, those girls were scary. They just came out of nowhere and attacked from every direction," said a team member. "Then they disappeared like ghosts...creepy, random-hair-colored ghosts."

"Then forget the rules," said Creepo. "Don't give the ghosts a chance. Now get your weapons loaded and let's get back out there."

The Green and Red Teams lined up on their respective sides. *Clang! Clang! Clang!* went the bell and the teams started to deploy.

Jonathan had divided Green Team into three groups of five people. They were planning a three prong attack: one group on the left, one on the right, and one in the middle. The two outer teams would form the prongs for a "pincer" attack, if needed.

Robert led the left team, Jonathan the middle, and Lindy the right hand side.

Robert's strike team was almost immediately eliminated. Some of the Red Team members had waited in ambush and caught them on the move. Robert and his four "casualty" team members quickly walked off the field with their guns held high over their heads. The Green Team strategy now had to change.

Green Team had originally planned to take out Red Team members in the front lines so they didn't have to worry about defending their barn and flag. Jonathan's team in the middle now had to pull back to protect their flag and barn more closely.

Lindy's team now switched to two roving groups, moving side-to-side to cover the battlefield as they moved forward.

Kimberly and Tim knelt patiently—well, Kimberly did at least—in the shade, next to a large oak tree. Kimberly's hair was turning blue. They heard a rustle in the bushes up ahead. Kimberly eagerly tapped Tim on the shoulder. Tim jumped in surprise, accidentally firing his paintball gun.

"Out!" came two enemy replies as they emerged from the bushes and headed for the non-battle zone.

"Good shot," whispered Kimberly.

"Thanks," Tim replied with a grin. "It's all in the wrist, you know."

Tim and Kimberly moved to a different location, slipping into a small gap between two boulders. The branches of a bush covered the gap. Kimberly's hair was now turning green in the partial shade. Tim, anxious to be on the go, slipped out into the small clearing beyond and was immediately pelted with five paintballs. He fell to the ground and called, "Out!"

Kimberly watched from her brush-hidden position as Tim rose to his feet with his gun over his head. He was suddenly shot three times more from point blank.

"Out!" Tim shouted. "I'm already out!"

Kimberly could see Tim was hurting. Three Red Team members stepped out from the bushes on the other side of the clearing and started questioning Tim about Green Team positions.

"I'm dead," Tim replied. "And besides, you're not supposed to shoot me this close."

One of the Red Team members laughed.

Kimberly aimed and fired rapidly, hitting all three of the Red Team members multiple times.

"Ouch!" called out the team members.

Kimberly, still in her hidden position, called out, "Which one of you shot my brother after he was already out?"

"It wasn't one of us," replied one of the Red Team members. "The guy that did it took off right after he did it."

"Okay, if they want to play that way," Kimberly said, "get your guns over your heads and get out of here. Your team is going *down!*"

The three opponents put their paintball guns over their heads and walked off.

"Tim, wait, I've got an ice pack for you," said Kimberly, still in her hiding position. Kimberly pulled the ice pack from her emergency pouch and said, "Here, catch," and tossed it over to him. "Get that ice pack working on your wounds and go find Robert in the safe zone and stick with him; I've got some work to do."

"Thanks," said Tim.

Once Tim was off the battlefield, Kimberly sprang into action. She hadn't noticed it but her ponytail holder had gotten snagged on one of the branches above her head and broken off. Her long hair, now waving down her back, was visible to anyone who might see her. Her hair had not the slightest trace of blue. Instead, it was turning redder and redder. Nobody messed with her brother and got away with it.

Kimberly was on a mission!

CHAPTER 9

Cleaning House

Kimberly believed in playing fair. She always tried to help people, especially the underdogs. She was a medic at heart and she also didn't like to see anybody hurt her younger brother. Yes, Tim could be kind of a goof and a pest sometimes but he was still her younger brother!

Kimberly checked her paintball ammunition level; the hopper was still nearly full. She scooted out of her current hiding place and carefully made her way back to the denser woods on the left side. She could hear someone quietly talking up ahead and ducked behind a large tree. Dropping to her hands and knees, she carefully looked around the trunk. There were two Red Team members there, advancing toward the Green Team barn. Kimberly let them pass and then opened fire, scoring several hits on both.

Kimberly jumped up and ran to another tree, leaving the "out" players to make their own way off the field.

Kimberly saw movement in the brush ahead. She hunched over and ran again, leaping over a large log as she went. Several paintballs whizzed by. She dropped to the ground and army crawled to get behind a large rock. Once there, she waited for a moment. The path seemed clear, so she got to her feet and ran for the protection of a large tree. Rounding the tree, she came face-to-face with Jonathan. Jonathan had to put his hand over her mouth to block her scream. They both ducked down.

"There's a group over there behind that wooden wall," whispered Jonathan. "They're going to head for our barn as soon as they get their guns reloaded. They took out three of my team."

"Tim got hit," Kimberly said. "I don't know where the rest of my group is."

"Why is your hair red?" asked Jonathan.

"I'm angry," said Kimberly. "One of the Red Team shot Tim at point blank range a bunch of times after he was out. It looked like it really hurt."

"You can bow out if you need to go check on him," said Jonathan.

"Right," said Kimberly, "and Red Team would probably shoot me in the back, too. No, let's go get them."

"Okay," said Jonathan, "let's go teach them that *nobody* messes with the Wright cousins."

"Now you're talking," Kimberly replied with a smile.

Kimberly and Jonathan quickly and quietly navigated around and behind their opponents stationed at the wood wall. At the last moment, one of them saw Kimberly. Kimberly jumped to her feet and charged, screaming *kamikaze* all the way.

Three surprised Red Team members turned toward Kimberly, saw her blazing red hair, and froze. Kimberly nailed them with paintballs. Jonathan caught two other enemies on the other side of a tree and put them out of the game, too.

One of the Reds, a college aged young man and already out, leveled his gun above his head and was readying to shoot Jonathan in the back from five feet away. Kimberly saw him, swung her gun, and nailed him with six direct hits. The player dropped his gun and threw his hands up in the air, angrily saying, "What was that for? I'm out, I'm already out!"

"For my brothers," Kimberly replied in full "momma bear" mode, "the one you already shot and the one you were just about to shoot. Now get off the field before I shoot you again!"

Staring at Kimberly's red hair, the young man quickly picked up his gun and left for the sidelines.

Jonathan and Kimberly made their way toward Red Team's barn. As they got closer to it, they saw Creepo, waiting in ambush, behind an old wooden wagon.

"You go left, I'll go right," whispered Jonathan.

The siblings split up and, running from tree-to-tree, worked their way around him. Jonathan was hit and put out of the game.

Peering around from behind a tree, Kimberly saw Jonathan heading for the sidelines. Kimberly hadn't noticed it before but Creepo wasn't alone; he had several guards protecting him.

One by one, Kimberly started taking out Creepo's guards. Finally, it was just down to Creepo and Kimberly. Creepo caught sight of Kimberly's red hair and turned to run. Kimberly paintballed him at full auto.

Creepo left the game wearing nine more paintball hits than he had had the round before. Kimberly captured the Red Team's barn and their flag. The game was over!

Kimberly quickly made her way over to the safe zone to check on Tim and the others. Her hair was turning more orange now rather than red. She spied the cousins at a picnic table, cleaning up their gear and exchanging "battle" stories with their friends on Green Team. There were Red Team members at nearby tables.

"Tim, how are you doing?" asked Kimberly when she got over to the Wright cousins.

"Okay," said Tim, still holding an ice pack on his back. "Thanks, Kimberly, this ice pack has really been helping."

Tim lifted the ice pack momentarily to show Kimberly his wound. She winced when she saw the red and blue welt.

"That one will take about two weeks to heal," said Kimberly.

"Yeah, but it was sure fun being out there," Tim said. "I can't wait until next time. Jonathan said you won the game for us."

"Yeah," Kimberly replied, "I mostly did it for you, though. I got the guy that shot you point blank; I'm going to report him to the owners. We don't need cheaters like that doing such dangerous things out here."

Kimberly was about to say something else but Tim quietly shushed her.

At a nearby table, the college-aged Red Team members were talking quietly among themselves. "I just got word the princesses might be at some kind of senior citizen community," said one of the group.

"That's it, then," said another. "Let's get on it before they can be moved again."

The group quickly gathered their gear and cleared out. The Wright cousins held a quick huddle once they were gone.

"Who were those guys?" said Jonathan.

"I don't know," Kimberly replied, "but one of them was called *Creepo*."

"Creepo was one of the guys who attacked Sarina at the college," said Jonathan in alarm. He turned to try to get a picture of them but they were gone.

Jonathan immediately phoned Sarina to warn her about what they had just heard.

"I was hoping we could stay closer to you guys," said Sarina, "but our intel has already warned us. We're preparing to move farther away, more remotely."

"I can't wait until this crummy war stuff gets over," said Jonathan. "You girls having to be on the run and hiding all the time. It's just not right."

"There are a lot of things that aren't right in the world right now," Sarina replied. "But we have to keep trying. We have to keep doing all we can and trust that God will help us."

There was a rustling sound in the background on Sarina's phone and then she said, "Jonathan, I have to go now. Take care, my special friend."

The phone clicked off before Jonathan had a chance to reply.

The next several days were challenging ones for the Wright cousins and the princesses. Every time it looked like things were finally going to settle down, something would come up and they'd have to dive in on another project or task.

For the Straunsees and their chaperones, it meant packing quickly and moving again. A different van came to pick them up and take them to a new destination. The van was accompanied by two unmarked security cars, one traveling in front and the other behind. All the Straunsees knew was that they were moving to another safehouse, *location unknown.*

At high school, the Wright cousins were facing schoolwork, schoolwork, and more schoolwork. Several of their teachers sprang surprise quizzes during their classes. One afternoon, the Wrights were sitting in the cafeteria, eating lunch with some of their friends.

"I just don't see why they have to test us on the names of all the songs written while looking at the prairie clouds and moonbeams," said Tim. He took another bite of his sandwich and continued, "That's not going to help us improve our flying or our paintball battles."

"Jonathan, what's wrong?" asked Robert, noticing that his cousin had been unusually quiet during their discussion.

"I'm worried about Sarina and the others," Jonathan replied in a whisper. "I haven't heard from her for a few days now. I hope they're okay."

"They'll be fine," said Robert. "Hey, what do you say we take our Grumman Duck airplane out and go flying this Thursday after school? We haven't even been to our airport hangar since we've been back."

Jonathan's face brightened. "That would be fun," he said. "I think we could all use a break."

"Yes," agreed Robert, "and what do you think about dropping in on the B-24 project?"

CHAPTER 10

The Boat

The Straunsee princesses and their chaperones were secretly moved to a new safehouse, this time far up in the mountains at Lake Pinecone. The house was about two miles out of town on the south side of the lake and was about one hundred feet from the water's edge. It was a wonderfully comfortable house with a big-windowed cupola on the roof, complete with mounted telescope, which gave an incredible view of the lake and its surrounding, pine-forested mountains.

In the basement of the house was a dry "boat storage" room. When not in use, the motorboat was cradled on a large steel cart with railroad-type wheels on it. A set of railroad tracks extended from the boat room down into the waters of Lake Pinecone. The tracks and their associated cable hoist allowed the occupants to store their boat securely and then run it down to the lake when they were ready to use it.

At their new safehouse, the three Straunsee girls settled into their regular education regimen by way of secured, online computer classes.

That morning, 13-year-old Maria Straunsee had woken up with a mean toothache. Mr. and Mrs. Olsen set up an emergency appointment and drove Maria into the town of Pinecone that afternoon to see a dentist.

Sarina and Katrina were doing schoolwork on their computers in the living room. Katrina's phone chimed, signaling her that she had received a text message. She gasped as she read it.

"What's wrong?" Sarina asked, noting her twin sister's concern.

"Look at this," said Katrina, holding her phone up so her sister could read it:

"Hurry, your lives are in danger. Take the safehouse boat to meet the Wrights at their island at the east end of Lake Pinecone. I have attached the digital direction file. The Wrights will signal you with a light to guide you in. IMPORTANT: Do not try to contact the Wrights, their phones have been compromised. The safehouse security guards are not to be trusted. We have just found out that they are working with your father's enemies. Do not contact anyone. Hurry to meet the Wrights!"

Shocked, Katrina and Sarina quickly went over to peek out the windows. They saw a guard at the driveway entrance. There was another guard at the upper fence.

Katrina checked her phone again and said, "It's from the Olsens and they told us to go by boat."

Rushing to the other side of the house, they peered out the windows overlooking the boat ramp. They didn't see any guards in that area. They quickly grabbed two of their small backpacks, loaded personal gear into them, and raced down the stairs to the basement. There, they loaded their gear into the boat in the boat room, threw on their coats, donned life jackets, and looked through the roll-up garage door's windows.

Still seeing no one, they opened the garage door. A gust of cold air hit them. They pushed the button to start the boat, on its cart, rolling down the steel tracks toward the lake. It was all electric so it made no noise except for a creak occasionally as the flanged, railroad-type wheels rolled down the tracks.

When the boat approached the water, both girls climbed aboard and took position in its cabin. The old railway cart went down into the water, stopped automatically, and the boat was soon floating on its own.

Katrina and Sarina were both familiar with boat operation because they had spent a lot of time scuba diving while growing up. One of the security guards came running around the far corner of the house, trying to stop them. Sarina fired up the boat's engine and off they went, speeding to meet the Wright cousins near the east end of Lake Pinecone.

The Straunsee twins had been travelling about seven minutes when they spied a boat behind them, heading in their same general direction. It was a much bigger and more powerful boat than the one the girls were in.

The boat seemed to be traveling about the Straunsees' same speed and would veer to the port or starboard every so often, so the girls didn't pay any attention to it after a while. They were moving at a pretty good clip and were very anxious to meet up with the Wright cousins.

Clouds were gathering over the mountains and the sky was beginning to darken. A wind began blowing out of the east, whipping up small waves and making the going a little bit choppier. The princesses adjusted their life jackets a little more tightly and kept going.

About seventeen minutes into their journey, with Katrina now at the helm, Sarina glanced back to see how the other boat was doing. To her surprise it was now less than half a mile away and was headed straight for them. To make matters worse, it seemed to be gaining on them!

"Floor it, Katrina," said Sarina, "that boat's after us!"

The girls rounded a small island, hoping to see the signal light from the Wright cousins that would guide them to safety. Up ahead, in the far distance, they could see a much bigger, pine-tree-covered island.

The clouds were getting ominously dark. It looked like it was going to rain. Off to their port side, the princesses could see gray streaks starting to come down from the clouds. It was hard to tell if it was rain, sleet, or snow. The wind was getting stronger and the boat's bow began pitching up and down as it hit larger and larger waves. There was a lightning bolt to the port side, several miles away. The girls couldn't hear the thunder because of the noise of their engine but they knew it was there.

They looked back to stern; the boat was still gaining on them.

A few minutes later, the boat had pulled alongside the princesses' boat as if it was going to race them.

"You'd better get aboard our boat," a young man at the railing called out through a megaphone. "This water's getting too dangerous for your little boat. We can take your boat in tow if you'd like."

Sarina waved them off but the boat stuck with them.

"It *is* getting pretty choppy," said Katrina, still at the wheel. "Maybe we should take them up on it."

"No way," Sarina said. "We don't know those people. For all we know, they could be some of Dad's enemies. Keep looking for the Wright's signal light."

Both boats sped on in the increasing storm. "We'll stick with you to make sure you get to your destination okay," called out the person in the other boat. "Where are you headed?"

The Straunsees could barely discern what the person had said. Sarina just pointed east. The larger boat pulled ahead and suddenly veered in front of the girls, cutting them off. Katrina yanked the steering wheel hard to starboard, to the right, to avoid them. She turned the boat tightly and set out east again. The larger boat, traveling faster, had to make a bigger loop and was soon on their stern again.

The boat was more aggressive this time. It came closer to their port side. "Stop your motor now and get onto our boat!" demanded a new person with the megaphone.

A shiver of shock went up and down Sarina' spine as she recognized the announcer. It was Creepo!

"Katrina, get away from them," warned Sarina. "They're the sleazebags that attacked me at the college."

Katrina turned hard to port. The boat shot past them. Katrina then acted like she was heading for the lake's south shore. Rain was starting to fall and lightning bolts were increasing in frequency and intensity around the mountains and lake. There was still no signal light from the Wright cousins!

"Come on, come on, Wrights, where are you?" said Sarina.

The large boat with several occupants turned and followed them. There seemed to be a struggle going on inside the bigger boat. A new person seized the helm. This time the large boat didn't slow as it approached the girls' boat; it charged directly at them.

The large boat rammed the Straunsees' boat at port stern. The small boat's bow shot high into the air. As the boat flipped over, Katrina and Sarina were thrown from the boat. They hit the water hard, skidding along the surface before finally slowing and plunging into the water. Their boat landed upside down.

Their lifejackets brought them to the surface as the larger boat spun around to find them. Katrina could smell fuel on the water. "Get away from the boat!" she called out to Sarina, still stunned and a few feet away from her.

Both girls started swimming as a flame suddenly shot up from their damaged boat. The fuel was on fire and the flames began spreading, burning the fuel as it spread out on the lake's surface.

The water was brutally cold. Katrina and Sarina were trying to make their way toward the lake's shore but it was still far away. Their life jackets were doing their jobs of keeping them afloat. Both girls were swimming strongly, making good progress, when a wall of flames flared up, encircling them. They were trapped!

"We'll have to take our life jackets off to swim under the flames," said Sarina. "Hang onto the straps, maybe we can yank them through the fire."

The temperature was getting unbearably hot as the girls undid the latches on their life vests and dove under the water. The fire's light cast an eerie glow underwater as the girls swam. Looking up, they could see an area free of flames and desperately swam toward it. By the time they surfaced, both of their life jackets were covered with burning fuel and had to be abandoned.

Creepo's boat turned about to see if the girls had survived. There was no bounty for dead princesses. He slowed the boat, circling round and round like a shark, as he and his crew scanned the water. Rain falling, fire and smoke filling the air, it was difficult for them to see anything. They tried their boat's bright spotlight but it did little good.

"There they are!" finally called out one of Creepo's gang. "I can see two people in the water on the other side of those flames."

Creepo, avoiding the fire, circled about, trying to get to the other side where the girls were.

The icy water had been stealing Sarina and Katrina's strength. Without their life jackets, they were having to propel their full weight through the water. Fire was everywhere and they kept having to dodge it. Their legs and arms were growing tired.

"Keep moving, Katrina, keep going," said Sarina, her lips now blue and shivering with cold.

Struggling, Sarina and Katrina were now about ten feet apart. A flash of flames shot up in front of them and they had to dive and swim under it. When they re-surfaced, they couldn't see each other.

"Sarina? Where are you?" called out Katrina.

Something monster-like clipped Katrina's foot, pulling her underwater. "Help me!" she screamed.

CHAPTER 11

Mysterious Find

The Wright cousins, even Tim, had been working very hard on their classes all week and were ready for a break. Their parents, who were out of town for the weekend, had given the cousins permission to travel to Lake Pinecone. The cousins' new electric air compressor had finally arrived and they were eager to get it installed in their submarine. The plan was to fly it out in their Grumman Duck seaplane, which could land on land as well as water. Realizing that several of the family cars were in the shop, the cousins had to use the big family motorhome to get to the airport.

When they arrived at the airport, the cousins rolled their airplane out of its hangar and parked their motorhome in the hangar for safe keeping. They loaded the air compressor into the lower compartment of their Grumman Duck, along with their luggage, went through pre-flight check-offs, and climbed aboard. Three of the cousins rode in the upper cockpit and two rode down in the passenger compartment. Jonathan was pilot. Take off went smoothly and they were free!

It was always an exciting adventure for the Wright cousins to fly in their old World War 2 airplane.

Moisture-ladened clouds were blowing in as the Wright cousins landed at Lake Pinecone and taxied over to their property's boat-and-airplane dock. The dock was in a small cove at the east end of the lake. The "property" included their secret submarine and underground submarine base. They had first discovered them during their *Great Submarine Adventure*.

Once they had the airplane secured at their dock, the cousins began the strenuous process of carrying their gear up the mountainside to the entrance of their base.

"I didn't see any rain listed in the forecast," said Robert.

"Me neither," Jonathan replied. "We'd better hurry and get this gear up to the tunnel."

"We're going to have to get that old mining tramway working again so we can get stuff up the hill easier," said Tim as he, Robert, and Jonathan struggled with the air compressor. "This thing is heavy."

"Yes," said Robert, "and camouflage the tram so people on the lake don't find it and break it."

It took two more trips up the mountainside for the cousins to get their luggage, food, and other gear up to the secret tunnel to their underground base. They were just in time because it was starting to rain. Unlocking the door and still using flashlights, they gratefully loaded their gear into the scoop-type, steel mine car just inside. They anxiously rolled the mine car along the track to their underground living quarters, where they unloaded their gear.

At the kitchen sink, Robert found an empty water bottle. He removed the cap, squirted some liquid dishwashing soap into it, filled it with water, and replaced the cap.

"What's that for?" asked Tim.

"I forgot my bubble-making bottle," said Robert.

"Oh," said Tim, "do you need the wand, too? I've got one in my back pocket."

"No thanks, I'm good," said Robert.

Robert and Jonathan walked down the stairs to the generator room, looked things over, and then started the generators.

"Okay," Jonathan called up the stairway to Tim, Kimberly, and Lindy, "we've got power. You can turn on the lights now."

With the flick of a switch, the cavernous old nickel mine, which had been turned into a World War 2 experimental submarine facility, changed from dark to light. Jonathan and Robert continued down the stairway to check on their submarine in the lower chamber. Tim soon joined them.

At the submarine room, Jonathan switched on the lights. Bright light shone down from high overhead in the huge room, bouncing off the water in front of the cousins and reflecting onto the solid rock walls and ceiling. Their submarine was docked to their left. The mine, from this point on to where it ran into Lake Pinecone, was filled with water. It provided the perfect secret passageway for the cousins to sail into the lake, fully submerged, without being seen.

The boys followed the walkway to the submarine's dock and crossed the gangway. As they stepped onto the submarine itself, they could feel it moving slightly under their feet.

Jonathan opened the crew hatch in the top of the conning tower and the three boys climbed down into the submarine. They also opened a deck access hatch and prepared the sub for its new air compressor. Soon, Jonathan, Tim, and Robert were lowering the air compressor down into the submarine.

"I'm really looking forward to putting this thing to use," said Robert. "The old compressor has been maxed out and this will definitely give us better air for the ballast tanks and torpedo tubes."

After twenty-five minutes of working, the boys had the compressor mounted inside the hull, electrically wired, and plumbed into the air lines. When that was done, the boys tested it out by switching it on and watching the pressure gauges.

"So far, so good," said Jonathan as they watched the tank and working pressure gauges rising.

"Maybe after dinner, we can take the submarine out into the lake to see how it performs with this increased air," said Robert.

"I was thinking the same thing," said Jonathan. "That way, we can try it out running on the diesel engine generator, too."

The boys shut down the compressor and listened for any sounds of air leaks. Hearing no "hissing," Robert retrieved his water bottle, shook it, and, using a rag, dabbed the water-soap mixture onto each joint of the air pipe they had just put together. Puzzled, Tim watched him.

"It will blow bubbles if there is a leak," explained Robert. "The soapy water works a lot better than just spitting on it."

Finding no leaks, the three boys closed up the submarine and headed back up to the kitchen area.

"Hey, that smells great," said Robert.

"Dinner's almost ready," said Lindy with a happy smile. "We're having beef stew and Crescent Rolls."

"Crescent Rolls?" said Robert. "One of my favorites!"

"Hey, save twenty of those rolls for me, please," said Jonathan. "I'll be right back."

Jonathan headed for the boys' bedroom to retrieve his lightweight coat from his duffle bag. As he was about to put the coat on, he heard a quiet, beeping sound. It sounded like it was coming from the right pocket but when he put his hand into the pocket, it was empty. He checked the left pocket and the chest pockets as well. All were empty and yet the beeping continued.

Jonathan felt along the coat and discovered something flat and boxy in the lining. Inspecting his coat's right-hand pocket more closely, he found a hole in the liner. The beeping continued but was growing fainter. Jonathan quickly worked the object, stuck in between the shell and the sewn-in liner, over toward the right pocket and got it out. He discovered it to be the emergency locating device he had used to find Sarina and Katrina at the mall in Flewdur, Gütenberg, during their *Trifid Castle* adventure. The fact that it was beeping meant trouble.

Each of the Straunsee princesses wore a lovely, delicate necklace with a stylized castle pendant on it. If one of the girls was in trouble, they could press a hidden button on the pendant and it would send their location for help. The fact that the beep was getting weak could only mean one thing: the batteries were failing.

Jonathan quickly opened the display cover on the locator. The screen inside showed a moving dot, giving location, speed, and distance from the locator.

"What's going on?" said Jonathan, studying the screen. The dot was moving slower than an airplane. It was out on Lake Pinecone and moving toward the cousins.

Jonathan hurriedly threw on his coat and rushed back into the kitchen. "Hey, you guys," he called out, "I just found this in my coat. The princesses are out on the lake and they're in trouble!"

CHAPTER 12

Help in Time?

"Lake Pinecone?" said Lindy.

"What can we do?" said Kimberly.

"We'll have to use the airplane or the submarine," said Robert. "I'll check on the weather outside."

Grabbing a flashlight, Robert ran to the entry of their base's tunnel.

While he was gone, Jonathan zoomed in on the locator's screen. "It looks like they're heading toward the island," he said. "I wish we could see what's going on."

Robert was soon back. "We're going to have to take the submarine," he said, still breathing hard. "There's lightning and thunder and it's raining cats and dogs out there right now."

"The sub it is," said Jonathan. "Let's get going!"

Robert grabbed a raincoat and said, "Lindy, can you bring the stew? I'm starving, we'll have to eat on board the sub."

"Sure," said Lindy. "I'll put it in a pressure cooker pot with a secure lid so it won't spill. Kimberly, give me a hand. We can grab some bowls—."

Within seven minutes, the Wright cousins had cast off the lines and water was closing in over the top of their submarine's conning tower. They were soon navigating their way through the flooded old mine tunnel on their way to the lake. They were running on battery power.

"We've just got to make a schnorchel for this thing," said Robert at the helm as he looked out the window ports in front of him.

"A what?" said Tim.

"Sorry, I've been reading up on German submarines again," Robert replied. "I meant a snorkel."

The cousins' submarine soon cleared the tunnel and was now traveling out into the lake, still fully submerged.

Jonathan, acting as sub commander, had the submarine brought up to "periscope" depth so they could look around before surfacing. The cousins didn't want word to get out about their submarine or their submarine base. Only they and their parents knew about it. It gave them the opportunity to explore the lake in private. It also kept people from trying to break, steal, or damage their equipment.

Using the periscope, Jonathan did a quick 360-degree scan of the horizon. "I don't see anything, he said with an urgency in his voice. "Let's take her up and see what's going on. We can travel faster on the surface."

The submarine was soon sailing swiftly through the water with just the top of its conning tower above the peaks of the waves. With the top conning tower hatch open for air, the Wrights were able to switch over to diesel power for more speed. Lindy and Kimberly, wearing raincoats, were using binoculars, scanning the horizon so they could see before being seen. A light rain was pattering on the sub and water around them.

Jonathan glanced at the locator. The beacon was still heading toward the cousins. If they kept to course, the Wright cousins would soon intercept them.

"I see a boat," said Lindy excitedly, "it's heading this way."

"Where?" said Jonathan and Kimberly at the same time.

"Directly west," said Lindy. "It just came out of a rain squall."

Jonathan grabbed a third pair of binoculars and joined in.

"I see it," said Jonathan.

"Me too," said Kimberly. "Why would they be coming out this way in this kind of weather?"

"There's a second, bigger boat. It just emerged from the rain, behind the first one," announced Lindy. "It looks like the second boat might be chasing the first one. It keeps messing with them."

"Robert," Jonathan called down into the hull, "give us full speed. Tim, we need minimum water drag. Get rid of some more ballast water. *Hurry!*"

Robert ran the throttles up. Tim switched the valves to begin pumping more air into the ballast tanks, forcing the heavy water out of them. There was a noticeable, rhythmic vibration resounding in the hull as the submarine plunged forward.

The sub sped along the surface in full sight of anyone who might be in the area. That didn't matter to the cousins right now, people were more important than things, and their friends were in danger.

Jonathan, Kimberly, and Lindy watched in horror as the second boat, a much larger and more powerful one, caught up with the first boat, passed it, and then cut in front of it. The bigger boat swerved to the side, almost as if it was playing tag. The smaller boat kept going straight toward the cousins' position.

The large boat appeared to pull alongside the small one and nudge it. The small boat swerved to the left and then bolted in a mad dash for the island. The large boat headed out away from the small one, as if it was going to leave it alone, and then turned and headed directly for the small boat. This time, instead of veering off at the last minute, it rammed the small boat. The small boat's bow shot high into the air and the boat flipped over.

The large boat sped past the small boat, slowed and turned back. There was a bright flash as the small boat erupted into flames. The large boat began circling the small, now sinking boat. Flames shot up from the water around the small boat and began to spread. The boat's fuel tanks had been damaged.

Jonathan's locator beeped once and stopped. He glanced at its blank screen. "No," he called out, looking back through his binoculars at the burning boat, "they can't...they mustn't die. O *please keep them safe!*"

Lightning bolts streaked across the sky as the submarine raced for the boats.

"Kimberly and Lindy, we'd better submerge," said Jonathan. "That boat might try to attack us, too. Robert and Tim, take us back down to periscope depth."

Kimberly and Lindy quickly climbed down the ladder. Jonathan followed and secured the hatch closed above them.

The cousins switched over to battery power and were fully submerged when they neared the burning wreckage several minutes later. Jonathan was glued to the periscope, searching, scouring the lake, for anything moving in the boat or the water. He studied the people aboard the large boat; they, too, seemed to be searching for survivors. He looked in the direction they were looking.

The other Wright cousins were anxiously peering out of the submarine's windows. They knew even seconds were critical. The girls might be injured. It was life and death. The water was too cold, the fire on the water, too dangerous.

"Tim," called out Jonathan, retiring the periscope, "take us down a few more feet so that boat doesn't hit our conning tower."

"Okay," Tim replied, manning the valves and filling the ballast tanks with more lake water.

The light from the burning boat and the fuel burning on the surface above them gave a surreal effect to the water below. The greenish-blue water glowed and flickered eerily.

Desperate, the cousins halted their submarine and switched on their forward external navigation lights. Seconds went by and then Lindy called out, "I think I see somebody in the water. Over closer to the burning boat."

"I see them," said Tim. "And there's a second one over there. It looks like there might be surface fire all around them. I only see two people."

Robert and Jonathan were already in their wetsuits.

"Tim, give us a hand at the diving chamber," said Jonathan.

"I'll take the helm," volunteered Lindy.

"Good idea," said Robert. "And Lindy, please get some warm stuff ready for us when we get back. I'm still hungry."

Donning swim fins, air tanks, and masks, Robert and Jonathan climbed into the sub's small diving chamber. Tim latched the watertight door after them and began the air pumping to pressurize the room.

Watching through a small window, Tim saw Robert and Jonathan each retrieve a light blue, 18-inch-wide, stingray-shaped underwater scooter from the chamber wall. The scooters were battery-powered and had two propellers.

Jonathan and Robert opened the bottom hatch and water began flowing into the chamber. Then, one at a time, they slipped down into the gurgling water. Seeing them clear, Tim headed for a window to watch Jonathan's and Robert's progress.

Once out of the submarine, Jonathan and Robert switched on their handheld, underwater scooters and, kicking powerfully with their fins, darted for the people in the water. Jonathan headed right and Robert headed left.

Avoiding some partially-submerged debris from the wrecked boat, Robert vectored toward a person struggling to stay afloat. It appeared to be a young woman. She was missing her shoes and was kicking with her feet, trying to keep her head above water. The fuel-covered water around her was burning, stealing her oxygen and giving her only a small window in the water's surface.

In his haste, Robert accidentally ran into Katrina's foot with his scooter. "Help me!" screamed Katrina. Robert surfaced immediately in front of her, nearly scaring her to death.

"Sorry," Robert called out, pulling his regulator from his mouth. "Katrina, It's Robert Wright, *follow me.*"

Robert handed Katrina his "safe second"—extra backup breathing regulator—which was connected by hose to his air tank. Grateful for the help, Katrina quickly slipped the regulator's mouthpiece into her mouth and clamped down on it with her teeth.

Robert signaled they were going to dive. Katrina nodded. Robert turned slightly and took hold of the underwater scooter with both hands. The princess grabbed his arm and braced herself for more cold water. Robert switched on the twin propellers and they headed underwater for the submarine.

Sixty feet away, Jonathan was rapidly approaching the second swimmer as fast as he could. He knew it was Sarina because she was wearing her favorite olive green coat. She was struggling, more than Katrina, because she had been hit on the forehead when the boat flipped over. Unable to swim anymore, she was sinking from the surface, bubbles trickling from her mouth and nose. Sarina Straunsee was *drowning!*

CHAPTER 13

50 Below

"No!" shouted Jonathan, almost blowing the breather out of his mouth. Rushing up behind Sarina, he caught her around the waist and pushed her toward the surface. Would he be in time?

Reaching the lake's surface, Jonathan fought to keep Sarina's head above water as he scrambled to inflate his rescue vest. He knew the Heimlich maneuver didn't work on drowned victims. If the princess's lungs didn't clear of the water in them, he would have to use CPR.

Sarina, her face blue from lack of oxygen, began gasping and coughing, spitting up water. She also began crying from the pain and fear of it all. As Sarina fought for her life, Jonathan struggled to hold onto her, trying with all his might to keep her afloat.

Sarina finally stopped coughing, but she was crying, crying for her life and what had almost happened to her. She turned around and hugged Jonathan around his neck, sobbing as she did. "I prayed you would come," she said to him. "I prayed you would come."

Sarina gasped for more breath, still crying. "Thank you," she said, "you've always...been there for me."

Jonathan pulled the breathing regulator from his mouth

and said, "I'm so glad you're okay."

Jonathan suddenly smelled gasoline fumes in the air and realized the fire was getting closer. "Sarina," he said, "we have to dive or we're going to get barbequed. Can you dive?"

Sarina glanced at the water apprehensively. She had almost drowned. She gulped, drowning her fear, glanced back at Jonathan and said firmly, "Where you go...I will go."

"Thank you," said Jonathan with relief, "Let's get out of here."

Jonathan quickly gave Sarina his extra regulator and put his personal one back in his mouth. He signaled for them to dive.

Sarina, on Jonathan's right, closed her eyes and clung tightly to Jonathan's right elbow with both of her trembling hands. She was cold, exhausted, and now fearful of the water. Jonathan knew he had to get her to warmth and safety fast. Five seconds after they dived with the scooter, the surface burst into flames.

Robert and Katrina were the first ones to arrive at the submarine. Robert helped Katrina up through the hatchway and into the submarine's partially-filled diving chamber. Robert followed her. The water in the chamber buoyed them up, making it easier for them to climb inside.

Robert got his head above the water, removed his breathing regulator, and asked, "Katrina, where's Maria?"

"Not here," Katrina replied, shivering. "She's in—in town with the Olsens."

"Thank goodness," said Robert. "We only saw two of you in the water. Jonathan's helping your sister."

Robert quickly pulled himself up the rest of the way into the diving chamber. He took off his weight belt and hooked it onto the wall. He then took off his diving tanks, secured them in a safety cabinet, and re-attached the scooter to the wall.

Jonathan and Sarina soon reached the submarine diving port and Robert helped pull them up, too.

Once they were all inside, they closed the bottom hatch and started the electric pump to remove the water from the small room. The two sisters hugged each other, shivering from cold and shock.

The boys worked quickly to stash their gear. As soon as the water was below the side door opening, Jonathan opened the door and he and Robert helped Sarina and Katrina into the main part of the sub.

Kimberly greeted them all with dry towels. "Thank goodness we found you," she said, handing out towels. "What happened out there? Never mind, you can tell us after you get warmed."

Jonathan and Robert took over working the submarine so Lindy and Kimberly could help the princesses. The boys stayed in their wetsuits, dried off as well as they could, and put on canvas deck shoes. They were eager to find out what was happening on the surface. They also wanted to get the identification on the large boat which had attacked Sarina and Katrina, so they could report it to the authorities.

"Robert, run us out about two hundred yards so we can take a look with the periscope," said Jonathan. "Tim, once we're there, take us up to periscope depth."

Rummaging through their emergency supplies, Lindy found a small duffle bag filled with some of her work clothes she used while working on the submarine. Sarina and Katrina were able to change into them in the submarine's bathroom. The clothes didn't fit perfectly but at least they were dry.

Kimberly and Lindy led the still-shivering girls into the middle of the submarine, the "salon" or "living room," where the table and benches were. After getting them wrapped in large red wool blankets and seated on a bench at the table, they served them each a mug of hot cocoa.

Smelling the sweet aroma of the chocolate, Jonathan called out, "Hot cocoa? Hey, can we have some, too?"

"Yes," said Robert, "that sure smells good."

"Make mine with lots of marshmallows, please," added Tim.

"Sorry, Katrina and Sarina outrank you guys right now," Kimberly replied. "But don't worry, we're heating up more."

"I demand a recount!" said Tim.

With the submarine at periscope depth, Jonathan, manning the periscope, began scanning the lake surface around them. He could see it was raining harder now. Lightning bolts were increasing in intensity. Jonathan could see smoking debris on the surface from the girls' boat, but the larger boat was nowhere to be seen.

As they sipped their hot chocolate, Sarina and Katrina were not only warmed but were given energy, too. Slowly, the color began returning to their faces; their lips were no longer blue. The girls were all eyes, looking curiously about them at their new surroundings.

"Jonathan," Sarina called forward, finally starting to feel more alive, "you never told me that you guys had a submarine."

"You never asked," Jonathan called back with a smile. "Pretty cool, huh?"

"Definitely," said Sarina and Katrina at the same time.

"Yeah, but you have to keep it secret, or we'll have to make you walk the plank," called out Tim.

"Timothy Wright, we'll do no such thing," Kimberly called back. She turned to Sarina and Katrina and said, "He is kind of right, though, in a way. We do need you to keep this top secret. Otherwise, well, people might find out and wreck it."

"Your secret is safe with us," said Sarina.

"We totally understand," Katrina said. "It's like our family secret passages and bunker you guys saw at our castle."

"Exactly," said Kimberly.

Grinning and glad to be finally able to share about their submarine, Lindy and Kimberly began the whole story. They told Katrina and Sarina about their property, exploration of Lake Pinecone, and the mysterious sea monster which was supposed to inhabit the lake. The princesses listened intently.

When she was feeling less shaky, Katrina said, "We need to get word to our father and the Olsens that we're okay."

"And to the police," said Lindy.

Jonathan did another sweep with the periscope. There didn't appear to be any other boats in sight.

The Wright cousins surfaced. Using an umbrella for shelter from the storm, atop the conning tower, Katrina tried to phone her father using Lindy's phone. Robert went up with her to keep lookout. The rain was still coming down hard.

"It's not the ritz," said Robert. "I hope to get an antenna set up again soon, so we don't have to stand out here in the rain."

"You guys are great," said Katrina, trying to call again.

Katrina couldn't get through to her dad, so Robert used the phone to call the Lake Pinecone Sheriff Department and make a report about the boat attack. They told him they would investigate it.

Katrina tried to call her father again; this time she got through. The phone connection was choppy because of the lightning storm.

"Hello Father," said Katrina, "we had a boat accident. We were in the water, but the Wright cousins rescued us. We're safe with Lindy and Kimberly."

"I'm so grateful to hear that," said King Straunsee. "Please thank them. With this war situation, I have been so worried about you girls. When I got the necklace emergency call—."

"Yes, don't worry, Father, we're safe now. I love you."

The phone call started cutting in and out, making it hard to hear.

"I love you, too, my beautiful daughter, Katrina," said King Straunsee. "We'll get this dangerous security situation straightened out. Stay where you are safe—."

The phone call dropped.

Katrina tried again but the phone showed no connection to the circuit. After five minutes of trying, they finally closed the top hatch and returned to the main part of the sub. The waves and storm were buffeting the submarine so the Wright cousins decided it would be best to dive below the waves again.

"Take us down about fifty feet," Jonathan instructed Tim. "Lindy, how is dinner coming?"

"Give us another ten minutes," Lindy replied.

Once below the waves, the submarine's ride turned to smooth again.

Lindy and Kimberly were just putting the finishing touches on dinner. With their royal guests on the submarine for the first time, the girls decided to go all out. They put a paper towel "tablecloth" on the table and rounded up silverware for everyone. After a blessing on the food and special thanks for the safety of Katrina and Sarina, they finally got to enjoy their supper.

"Lindy, your beef stew and these Crescent Rolls are incredibly good," said Katrina. "How did you do it?"

"Yes," said Sarina, "I'd like to get your recipes for our Straunsee Castle chef."

Lindy blushed from all the attention. "My mom and I are actually putting together a recipe book that includes both the Crescent Rolls and the beef stew. I'm so glad you like them."

"Hot-buttered Crescent Rolls," said Robert. "That recipe alone will make your book sell a million copies!"

"And we get to enjoy them in our secret submarine," said Jonathan.

"Yes," said Sarina with a smile, "this is truly wonderful."

With the fury of the storm continuing a mere fifty feet above them, the Wright cousins, Sarina, and Katrina enjoyed a delicious, warm meal beneath the waves. They were all, for now, safe and alive, where no enemy could reach them.

CHAPTER 14

Return

After the dinner, Sarina and Katrina continued to rest and recover. The Wright cousins sailed the submarine back to their property and into the underground base without incident. Once they surfaced in the old mine, they disembarked, and the boys worked on securing the sub.

"Follow us," said Lindy, and she and Kimberly led Sarina and Katrina up the stairs to the main living level.

"This is like our bunker at Straunsee Castle," said Sarina.

"Except you guys get the good cartoon channel there," Tim called out after them.

"You girls must be pretty wiped out," said Lindy as they entered the girls' large bedroom. "We can show you around in the morning."

"Thank you," said Sarina. "That cold lake water really takes it out of you."

"That and everything else you girls went through today," said Lindy.

The girls set up two extra cots, complete with warm sleeping bags and pillows. Lindy and Kimberly gave Katrina and Sarina some of their extra clothes so they would have fresh clothes to wear in the morning.

By the time the boys came up from securing the submarine

and had it connected to the battery charger, the girls were all fast asleep. The boys, too, tired from the labors of the day, headed to the boys' bedroom and hit the hay.

They all slept well that night, all except for Tim. He dreamt the boat he was sailing on sunk in a big hot chocolate ocean. He had to climb onto a giant marshmallow to save himself. And then he got really hungry. Should he eat his marshmallow boat or keep floating on it? When he woke up, he was still licking his lips and his pillow was gone.

"Rats," said Tim, "that's my third pillow this week!"

After breakfast, the Wright cousins showed Sarina and Katrina around the underground base. Kimberly examined Sarina's wounds and deemed it should be okay for the girls to explore the surface of the property above them. The bruise on Sarina's forehead was looking better.

Leaving the others in the kitchen, Jonathan showed Sarina the tunnel that led to the surface of the property. Once outside the tunnel, they found that the storm had cleared out and the rain had left everything looking shiny, sparkling, and new.

"It's so beautiful out here," said Sarina as they walked amongst the tall pine trees. "The air is so fresh and clean. I can see why you all like it so much."

"Especially after a storm," said Jonathan.

They walked out to a prominent point which overlooked the lake and sat down, side-by-side, on a big granite rock. The lake was blue and shimmering in the sunlight. The breeze was cool but delightful. The sky an incredible, deep blue. The sun was warming.

They sat there, quiet, enjoying just being together, looking at the beautiful mountains and lake before them.

"Jonathan," said Sarina quietly, "what are your feelings about kissing?"

Jonathan chuckled slightly and said, "Well, I..."

Jonathan thought about how he might tell her his feelings, the way he felt deep down inside. He really enjoyed being with Sarina. Why, ever since they had met at Fort Courage during their *Case of the Missing Princess* adventure, his life had been different. His life had been changed for the better. Sarina was his best friend now. He didn't want to say the wrong thing or embarrass her. He really, truly liked, loved, this girl who was sitting beside him. And yet he needed to tell her how he felt and why he hadn't kissed her yet. It was hard to put into words.

Sarina noticed Jonathan's silence. She glanced at him briefly and then out at the lake again. Jonathan's cheeks had blushed slightly. Sarina didn't mean to embarrass Jonathan, her dearest friend in all the world. She wanted, needed, to know where they stood and how they might move forward in life. How things might work out for their possible future.

"If you don't want to talk about it right now," said Sarina quietly, "it's okay. We just need to discuss it sometime."

"Now's good," said Jonathan, clearing his throat slightly. "I...years ago, I went to a class on dating and marriage relations. The speaker talked about how he had met his wife and how special she was to him. He talked about becoming friends first and sweethearts second. He also talked about holding hands and kissing and things. He said that what had made a huge difference in his life was that he had made up his mind, when he was still young, that he wasn't going to kiss a girl until they were engaged to be married. He said that kissing was the easy part. That we first need to build the respectful, friendly, kindness part of the relationship to make it last forever. I want that for me, too. I want a forever marriage. I've decided to save kissing until when I'm engaged to be married. I know it's not for everybody, but kisses mean too much to me. I want to save the most sacred part of human love for after I'm married."

Sarina was quiet for a moment and then said, "That's one of the things I love about you, Jonathan Wright. You're not like so many of the other guys. You think things through. You plan for success. You're not out to take advantage of my being a female, my young womanhood, or get me to do things I shouldn't do, wrong things. It makes a girl, me, feel safe when I'm around you. Thank you. I don't know what the future holds but I'm hoping it includes being with you. I'm comfortable with you. We're a good team. Life is so much better when we're together. I will support you in your goal of not kissing until we're...you're engaged to be married...if you'll support me, too. We'll save the sacred."

"Granted," said Jonathan with a big, relieved grin as he glanced at Sarina. "And what a kiss that will be! I mean, well you know."

Sarina nodded, blushing as she smiled, and leaned her head against Jonathan's shoulder. The world was even brighter now, the future more hopeful, their friendship more precious and dearer. Life was good, *very good*.

The Wrights and the princesses spent most of the day at the property. For lunch, they picnicked on a pretty spot overlooking the shimmering lake. After their ordeals of the day before, they were grateful for the peace they felt in the mountains and the chance to catch their breath.

They explored the old mine buildings and the tramway, too, and found some new diggings the Wright cousins didn't even know about.

Later in the afternoon, Jonathan's phone beeped with a text message. "Jonathan, this is the Olsens," it said. "Please bring the princesses and meet us at your airport hangar."

The message went on to set up the time for meeting.

Jonathan told the others of the request. It was like pouring ice water on their otherwise very wonderful day.

"But Father told us to stay where we are safe," said Katrina.

"Yes," added Sarina, suspiciously, "and how do we know this text is actually from the Olsens. The message sent to us yesterday was a trap and almost got us killed. Jonathan, let me see that text, please."

Jonathan handed his phone to Sarina. Sarina studied the text closely, deep down hoping it was fake.

"It is from the Olsens," Sarina said finally with disappointment in her voice. She glanced at Katrina. "They included their own secret identification code in it."

"How?" said Tim.

"Sorry, Tim," said Sarina, "it's secret agent stuff."

"Oh," said Tim with a quick salute. "Stiff upper lip and all that."

"Tim, you are such a goof sometimes," said Kimberly with a slight grin.

"Thank you, thank you," said Tim. "But flattery will get you nowhere."

Jonathan glanced skyward for a second and then said, "Well, we'll need daylight for our flight back home. We'd better get going."

"Yes," said Sarina, glancing at Jonathan. "Sorry, I guess we'll have to. It's been so nice being with you guys."

"You, too," said Jonathan and the rest of the cousins.

The teenagers quickly packed their bags, secured the steel doors, and headed down to the airplane. When they got there, they found muddy footprints on the dock where their plane was secured. They had been washed by the rain so it was hard to tell if they were made by people or by animals.

The cousins quickly looked over their plane to see if there was any damage. They couldn't find any, so they loaded their gear and climbed aboard. After starting and letting their engine warm up, they taxied out onto the main lake. The waves were calmer this morning and it made their takeoff run much smoother.

"Here we go," called out Jonathan.

Sarina was sitting in the middle cockpit seat behind Jonathan with Robert in the back; the rest were riding—somewhat scrunched—in the passenger compartment below.

Once in the air, Jonathan circled to gain altitude and show Sarina a beautiful view of Lake Pinecone. They were wearing flying caps with radio headgear so they could communicate without having to yell over the noise of the plane's powerful engine.

"It's fun to see this whole lake region. It's amazing down there," said Sarina. "What a beautiful world we live in."

"We're the Wrights in de-skies," spoke up Tim down in the passengers' compartment. "Get it, guys, you know, the Wrights in *the skies*. We'll keep the princesses safe."

"Right!" said everybody at the same time.

The cousins soon left Lake Pinecone and headed toward their home airport. The air was crisp and clear as they flew along.

The airplane suddenly shook. Jonathan glanced at his gauges.

"What's wrong?" asked Sarina as the plane shook again.

"I'm not sure," Jonathan replied.

The plane shuddered again. Puffs of white smoke came out of the exhaust pipes. The engine started to cut out and then started up again.

Robert looked over the side and spied a flat area below them with a road running through it.

"Jonathan, there's a place down there if we need to land," Robert called out.

"I see it," Jonathan replied.

The engine began sputtering again and the Grumman Duck began losing altitude.

Jonathan set the flaps to slow the plane for landing. The engine sputtered, emitting more white smoke, followed by more regular, black exhaust. They started to gain altitude again as the engine worked hard. It sputtered again, this time losing fifty feet of altitude before the engine ran smoothly again. Then they dropped again.

"That does it," said Jonathan, "we're going to have to land down there. We can't take a chance and lose power over the forest.

"You can do it," said Sarina, patting him on the shoulder. "You've got this."

Jonathan brought the plane down toward the lonely road, keeping the nose up to slow the plane. The engine sputtered again, blowing out puffs of white smoke and then black soot.

Jonathan was just about to touch down when the engine smoothed up and gained full power. Gunning it, he angled the nose toward the sky and took off again. The engine was running smoothly without a flaw now.

"What was wrong?" asked Sarina.

"Could be some water in the fuel filter or something," said Jonathan.

"Probably from that storm last night," said Robert. "Or those muddy footprints."

"True," said Jonathan. "We'll have to have the mechanic check it out when we get home."

The engine ran without flaw the rest of the way to the airport. Talking with the control tower, Jonathan got clearance to land. The sun was just setting as they touched down and slowly taxied over to their hangar.

Letting the engine cool, the cousins opened the hangar doors and rolled the plane inside.

"You did alright, old girl," Jonathan said, stepping back from the plane.

"What?" said Sarina, who was standing beside him.

"Sorry," Jonathan replied, blushing slightly, "I was talking to the airplane."

"Jonathan talks to a lot of things," Tim said. "Why, just yesterday, he was talking to the submarine and then his hat, too. He's a very conversant guy."

"Thanks for the enlightenment, Timothy," said Jonathan.

"Glad to help," said Tim with a grin. "I'm just here to be conversant...with."

Kimberly eyed Tim suspiciously and said, "Tim, was *conversant* one of your spelling words for this week?"

"Yeah, well, actually it was," Tim said. "Our teacher said we could get extra credit for each time we used *conversant* in a sentence, you know, *conversantly*."

"Speaking of being *conversant with*," said Kimberly, elbowing Tim. "How about you being *conversant with* helping us carry our luggage over to the motorhome."

"If I did," said Tim, "then that would make me very conversant with carrying luggage. That works for me; I could get fifty extra credit points. I just have to write down the sentences I was conversant with. And if I say them in front of Lindy, she could help me remember them, right?"

The cousins carried their luggage over to the motorhome.

"I thought the Olsens were supposed to meet us here," said

Tim.

Jonathan looked at his watch and said, "We're about fifteen minutes early."

Robert and Tim unlatched the security latches on the automatic garage door to get ready to drive the motorhome out of the back of the hangar. They heard a rumbling noise outside and Robert went to see who it was. Glancing out the window in the smaller personnel door on the side wall, he saw several large pickups pulling up. "Oh no!" he said, "that looks like trouble."

Robert turned to the others and called out, "Hey you guys, we've got company and it doesn't look good!"

CHAPTER 15

Rough Ride

"Serious?" Jonathan called back.

"Yes!" said Robert. "And it's definitely not the Olsens. It looks like those guys from the paintball games!"

"I definitely don't want to get more conversant with those guys!" said Tim. "Hey, that's another ten points."

"Everybody, get into the motorhome!" Jonathan cried out.

They ran for the motorhome and climbed aboard just as a side window on the hanger was broken and a metal object was thrown in, followed by a second one. Gas started spraying from them.

"It looks like tear gas," called out Robert to Jonathan in the driver's seat. "Let's get out of here!"

Robert pushed on their remote-control garage door opener and the door started lumbering upward. Jonathan fired up the motorhome. As soon as the door was high enough, they drove out.

The roaring motorhome caught Creepo and his gang by surprise. Unable to stop it on foot, they dashed to their pickups to give chase.

Jonathan rapidly drove the motorhome off the airport property and onto the narrow, two-lane highway which headed the back way toward town. Creepo's gang sped after them in four stolen, full-sized pickups.

Jonathan could now see the pickups in his rearview mirror; they were gaining on him.

"Jonathan, can't we go any faster?" called out Kimberly.

"Sorry, 63 miles per hour is the best we can do," Jonathan replied, "unless Robert has come up with some kind of rocket boosters."

"I wish," said Robert, "that chemistry class has been keeping me too busy."

The front pickup, going well over 90 miles per hour, soon caught up with the cousins and was trying to pass them. The other pickups were not far behind. Jonathan swerved side-to-side, trying to cut them off and stay in front of them.

The passenger in the lead pickup reached out of his door window and started shooting a pistol at the motorhome's rear tires.

A second pickup pulled up alongside the first, this one traveling in the wrong lane. The passenger had a rifle and started shooting at the motorhome, too.

Keeping their heads down, the cousins in their motorhome kept driving as fast as they could. It wasn't looking good.

"Pull up closer," said the rifleman. His driver pulled closer to the motorhome and several more shots were fired.

"We're in big trouble," said Kimberly as bullets whizzed overhead. "Guys, we've got to do something!"

"Tim, let's finish the water cannon we were making for our new business," said Robert.

Robert and Tim hurried over to the wiring harness. Jonathan kept swerving as Robert and Tim worked, making it hard for them to stay on their feet.

"Tim, hang onto these wires while I figure out where they go," said Robert.

Robert looked at the schematic diagram for the water pump wiring and said, "I think the red goes to this terminal over here."

The other cousins and the princesses were watching the pickups following them.

"Um, black wire," said Robert, "hand me the black wire. Hey Jonathan, let me know when we're going to be turning."

"Okay," said Jonathan, "we're turning to the right and then the left and then the right again. Those guys in the pickups are just trying to kill us, that's all."

"Yellow wire," said Robert, retrieving a wire nut to attach it.

"Yellow wire," said Tim.

The motorhome swerved sharply, throwing Tim and Robert against the water cannon pipes.

"Ouch," said Robert. "Jonathan?"

"Hurry up and get that water cannon working," Jonathan replied. "They're getting out some heavier artillery."

"Yes," added Sarina from the back. "They just shot out one of the back windows."

"The other white wire," said Robert. "We have to connect all the whites together."

"I've just got to ask," said Tim. "Do we have any water in the water tank?"

"Yes," replied Lindy and Robert at the same time.

Lindy added, "We were getting ready to water my mom's garden."

"Robert?" called out Jonathan. "These guys are getting ready to shoot something big at us."

"We're just about done," Robert replied. He quickly gathered the wire-nutted wires, bundled them together, and pushed them into a metal conduit box.

"Okay, Tim, flick the switch," said Robert. "Let's see if we've got this right."

Tim turned on the electrical switch. They watched the water pressure gauge rise.

"So far, so good," said Robert. "Okay Tim, let's try it out."

Since their *Secret Agents Don't Like Broccoli* adventure, the Wright Cousins had kept their 8-wheel-drive armored car camouflaged as a motorhome. Robert and Tim climbed up into their armored car's turret.

Katrina had recognized the interior once she was in it.

The armored car was set up for nine people. Each person had on their safety helmets with earphones and microphones. It gave them communications and protected their heads from hitting the strong armor. The original turret cannon's breech had been removed, per government regulations, and the cousins were using its barrel as a water tube.

Tim pushed a button to raise an exterior panel on the outside of the motorhome at turret level.

"What's going on?" said a driver in one of the pursuing pickups.

Robert worked the controls for turning the turret back and forth. Glancing at the viewer in front of him, he began tracking the nearest pickup. Robert squeezed the trigger but nothing happened. He tried it again. "Now what?" he said. "Tim, the solenoid switch isn't working. We'll have to bypass it and have you do it manually with the ball valve. I'll tell you when."

Robert lined up the sights again on the nearest truck. "Okay, Tim, let her rip!"

Tim pushed on the ball valve's handle, rotating the valve's inside mechanism 90 degrees.

Water shot out from the cannon, hitting the truck's

windshield and splashing off.

"Don't worry about it," said the pickup's driver, greatly relieved. "It's only water."

"What do those jokers think they're trying to do?" said the passenger as he aimed at the motorhome's tires.

Robert and Tim tried the water cannon again. In the shadows of the motorhome, water just trickled out of the end of the barrel like a garden hose.

"Something's wrong," said Robert desperately. "The wiring must not be right."

The first sign of water had made the trucks pull back but now they were emboldened. Like wasps on a helpless victim, the trucks started attacking the motorhome more viciously.

One truck came up and rammed the motorhome from the side to force it off the road. Jonathan cranked the armored car's steering wheel and pushed back; the 12.8 ton armored car hit the pickup so solidly that it sent the pickup swerving off the road and into the muddy farm field beyond.

Robert quickly studied the wiring schematic again. Lindy came over to help him work through the puzzle. She glanced at the diagram and then back at the wiring.

"The grounds are wrong," said Lindy. "Our armored car uses 24-volt positive."

"Oh, I forgot about that," said Robert. "I hope I haven't burned up the electronics."

Robert re-routed the wires and quickly matched them up differently. "There," he said, "let's try that."

Robert and Tim got back into position. Robert touched the trigger switch for just a second. This time it worked!

Robert aimed the water cannon at the nearest pickup truck behind them and squeezed the trigger. The high pressure waterjet hit the front of the pickup and blew its radiator to shreds. Steam and antifreeze sprayed all over the truck's windshield.

Robert raised the cannon slightly and squeezed the trigger again, hitting the truck's engine hood release. The hood flipped up, smacked into the windshield, breaking its hinges and flying over the cab of the truck. In their desperation to get out of the way, the truck veered off the road and into a muddy field.

The fields on both sides of the narrow highway belonged to Mr. Akio. He had recently plowed them. Since then, they had been flood-irrigated and rained on. By now, it was excellent, slimy mud. The pickup sped into the field 300 feet and sunk down to its axles. There was no way the gooey, gloppy mud would let go of the rudely trespassing truck or its passengers.

"All right," said Tim. "Let's try that again!"

Tim raised more side panels on the modified motorhome. Robert aimed at a second pickup. This time the water blew off a side mirror, cracked the windshield, and blew off the driver's door. The truck sped off the road and into the muddy fields beyond.

Creepo's pickup was the last truck still in pursuit and he showed no signs of giving up.

"Robert, we're almost out of water," Tim called out. "We've got to make this one count!"

Creepo's truck pulled up behind the lefthand corner of the motorhome. He smirked as he stuck his assault rifle out the passenger window and opened fire. The bullets ripped into the motorhome but with surprisingly little effect.

Creepo looked at his assault rifle and called out, "That thing must be built like a tank. Sid, take us closer."

Creepo's driver pulled up to within ten feet of the back of the motorhome and Creepo fired again. Bullet holes began appearing in the metal trim and siding.

"They wanted the princesses alive," called out Sid.

"Our government will pay for whatever we give them," said Creepo angrily. "That princess burned me once; she will never do that again."

Creepo opened fire again. Some of his bullets hit the turret of the armored car.

"I'm tired of that creep messing with us," said Jonathan. "Robert and Tim, get him! *This time he's going down!*"

CHAPTER 16

Break

The pickup tried to pull out around the motorhome and pass it, but Jonathan blocked it.

Robert aimed the water cannon at the left front of the pickup and squeezed the trigger. The waterjet tore through the truck's grill and hit the air intake of the truck's engine. Water was sucked into the powerful engine and fed to the cylinders. Intense pressure suddenly built up inside the engine as the water didn't ignite. The engine blew up, sending the cylinder heads, pistons, and broken connecting rods flying through the air, whipping up the engine hood and smashing it against the cab. Trying to avoid the shrapnel, the pickup driver yanked the steering wheel to the right. He lost all power, and the pickup truck flew off an embankment and into the gooey, muddy world beyond.

Creepo's truck bounced twice and slid through the gooey mud, coming to a stop several hundred feet from the road. Just after it stopped, the truck's airbags went off, smacking Creepo and his driver in the faces like a cannon shot. Mr. Akio's fields were now the proud owners of a fourth pickup truck and its occupants.

Jonathan slowed and stopped the motorhome-covered-armored car in the right lane so they could watch the truck people and make sure none of them got away.

"It worked," said Robert, punching his fist into the air and nearly hitting the ceiling of the turret, "it really worked!"

Jonathan turned on the emergency flashers, climbed out of the driver's seat, and made his way back to the large personnel compartment in the rear of the armored car. He and Sarina quickly got on the phone to contact family and law enforcement.

"This is Jonathan Wright of the *Wright Princess Protection Service*," Jonathan spoke into the phone. "We need you to pick up some spies and assassins that have been trying to kill friends of our country."

"We're friends of Kimosoggy," added Robert.

"Kimosoggy?" said the other person on the line. "*We'll be right there!*"

"Wow," said Robert in a whisper, "it works every time."

After getting off the phone, the Wright cousins lowered the side panels on their motorhome to re-disguise their armored car.

"Now this is the Wright disguise," said Jonathan, patting the old motorhome. "We need to give you a name."

"How about Fred?" said Tim.

"Tim, that's the name of our submarine," said Kimberly.

"Oh yeah," said Tim.

"How about *Wheels*?" said Lindy.

"I like that," said Jonathan, "And each letter can stand for something, like *Water, Helper...*"

"*Extra, Emergency*," added Kimberly. "Now for the LS."

"*Leute, Shelter*," said Katrina.

"*Leute* means *People* in German," Sarina explained.

"Good," said Jonathan. "Motorhome, we do hereby dub thee *Wheels*. All in favor, say *aye*."

"Aye," came six replies.

"And may the *water* Force be with you...*always*," added Robert, patting the old motorhome. They all laughed.

In less than five minutes, law enforcement helicopters were flying overhead and ground units were arriving with flashing lights and sirens blaring.

Teams of FBI agents and sheriff deputies pulled up in patrol cars accompanied by two large, suspect retention vans. One-by-one, the members of Creepo's gang were extracted from the mud, handcuffed, and read their rights. Creepo and his driver had to be picked up by helicopter because no car could make it through the mud to get them.

Sarina, Katrina, and the Wright cousins stood beside their motorhome, watching as members of Creepo's gang were led to the awaiting detention vans. Sarina had her hand slipped around Jonathan's elbow.

"Princess, you missed out," Creepo called out sarcastically as he was led by in handcuffs.

"No, *you are* missing out," Sarina called back firmly. "You've attacked and tried to kill us. The way you're going, you'll *never* have a wife or family. You'll just be a lonely, decrepit old man. Let me give you a clue, Creepo: *Evilness never was happiness.*"

After all the gang was secured, one of the officers came over to talk with the group. "Which one of you is Robert Wright?" she asked.

"I am," said Robert standing up straighter.

"I need to speak with you for a second."

Robert left Katrina's side and went over to talk with the officer.

"I understand you have connections with a mutual friend of ours," the officer said.

"Who is that?" said Robert.

"Codename: Kimosoggy," the woman replied.

"Oh, yes," Robert said.

"Thank him, for the service, and tell him to keep up the good work."

"Thank you, I will," said Robert, blushing slightly. "I will."

"Thank you," said the officer, and she turned and walked over to her SUV, climbed in, and drove away.

The Wright cousins and the Straunsees were left all alone in the quiet evening. The stars were out and shining brightly.

"Well, what about that," said Jonathan. "Creepo's gang is finally gone."

"Thank goodness," said Sarina.

"It's so peaceful here," Katrina said. "Away from the city lights."

"I'm hungry," said Tim. "Let's go get something to eat."

Kimberly elbowed him.

"Hey," said Tim, "what was that for?"

"Interrupting our peace and quiet moment," Kimberly replied.

"Wow, there goes a shooting star," said Lindy.

"Where?" said Robert.

"Over there, to the northwest," pointed out Lindy.

"I'm hungry," said Tim.

"Tim, enjoy the moment," said Kimberly.

"You know, I'm getting kind of hungry, too," said Sarina.

"Then let's go get something to eat," said Jonathan. "What kind of food would you like?"

"Wait a minute," said Tim, glancing at Jonathan and Sarina and then back to Kimberly. "Kimberly, I just said that. Never mind, I get it, *she's a princess.*"

"She's not just a princess," Kimberly replied, "*she's his*

princess...his special and best friend. Someday, you'll figure it out."

"Mush," said Tim, "mush and smooshies. Let's go get some hamburgers and vanilla shakes, this princess protection stuff makes me hungry."

They all climbed back into their motorhome and back down into the armored car through the top personnel hatches. Once everyone was seated and seat-belted, Jonathan started up the big diesel engine and they drove off in search of a fast-food restaurant.

The Wright cousins' motorhome was too big for the restaurant's drive-thru lane, so they ordered remotely and parked off to the side.

Robert and Tim walked over to the restaurant to get the food for their group. They were just coming out the door with bags filled with hamburgers, fish sandwiches, onion rings, salads, and strawberry, chocolate, and vanilla shakes. A man held the door open for them and said, "Look at that poor motorhome over there. And I thought my motorhome back home was in rough shape."

"Could be termites," said Tim, "I hear they're really bad this time of year."

"Termites?" said the man. "I didn't realize that was a problem. I'll have to watch mine more closely. Hmm, I wonder if the dollar store sells termite spray?"

Robert and Tim quickly returned to their motorhome and climbed down through the top hatches into the armored car to join the others.

"Anybody want some pickles and tomato?" asked Tim. "I forgot to tell them to leave them off."

"Sure," said Jonathan and Sarina at the same time.

"Pass the ketchup, please," said Robert.

"Does anybody know where the Ranch salad dressing is?" asked Kimberly. "Tim, could I have one of your onion rings, please?"

"Hey, Robert and Tim, while you were in the restaurant, we got word from Dad," Jonathan said. "They've arranged for a safe house for us to stay at tonight. They downloaded it onto our armored car's navigation system."

"Sounds good," said Robert, sipping his vanilla shake through a straw. "Whew, this is kind of cold, maybe we should start up the heater or something."

The food tasted great, and the cousins and princesses were soon feeling much better.

"'Full tummy, nice and warm, go to sleep,'" said Lindy with a smile. "That's how Mom usually says it."

When Jonathan started up the armored car and pulled back out onto the street, a digital map appeared on the vehicle's navigation screen to show him where to go.

Jonathan wasn't totally familiar with the area, but he followed the directions as shown. Curious, he pulled onto the road as instructed. The armored car seemed to be acting a little strangely.

CHAPTER 17

Doors

The words "New Safehouse Parking Instructions" appeared on the screen. "Pull into residence's tall garage on right side of house to secure motorhome."

"Are you sure we want to do this?" asked Kimberly from the personnel area in the armored car.

"The message has Dad's security code," said Jonathan. "We can always back out if we need to. We've been through a garage door before with this thing, remember?"

As they approached the house, the large garage door began to open. Jonathan pulled into the driveway and slowly into the garage. There were shelves along the sidewalls, but the bay was plenty wide. The garage didn't seem deep enough for their long motorhome. Not wanting to hit the back wall, Jonathan carefully inched forward to get the vehicle entirely within the garage.

"It's too close," said Robert, "I'll get out and direct you."

Robert climbed out of the motorhome and, with flashlight in hand, motioned for Jonathan to continue forward.

Jonathan drove forward and the front of the motorhome accidentally bumped the forward wall. To their astonishment, a large, vertical crack appeared in the middle of the wall and the wall began to move. The wall was made up of two large doors and they began swinging open, away from the front of the motorhome, revealing a large, dark, secret tunnel.

A door opened on the side wall common with the house and light flooded into the garage, silhouetting a person wearing an apron.

"Oh, dearie me," the person said, "do you want me to park that thing for you?"

"Great Aunt Opal?" said Robert, recognizing the voice. "What are you doing here at our safehouse?"

"My dear boy, my house is *always* safe," Aunt Opal replied. "I take great precautions to make sure it stays that way. Tell your family to park in the concrete tunnel so we can still use the garage, please."

"Oh, yes, sure," said Robert.

Jonathan soon had the motorhome pulled into the underground tunnel. It was made of steel reinforced concrete and had been dug into the hill immediately behind the garage.

"My husband, Floyd, built it years ago during the Cold War," said great Aunt Opal. "It makes for a good root cellar when I don't need to park in it. Keeps my long-term food storage nice and cool."

The rest of the cousins and Sarina and Katrina soon emerged from the motorhome and were standing in a group, looking at their new surroundings.

"Well, please, won't you come inside where it's warmer?" said great Aunt Opal.

Jonathan introduced the princesses to Great Aunt Opal and she to them, and then Aunt Opal led them all into her home. "This is one of my rental properties," she explained. "Please, make yourselves comfortable."

Timothy saw great Aunt Opal eyeing his shoelaces. "They're tied," he said with a grin.

"Good, Timothy," said Aunt Opal, "we wouldn't want you to trip and fall over untied shoelaces, now, would we?"

"No, no, definitely not," Tim replied. "Loose shoelaces are trip-causers."

"Good for you, Timothy," said Aunt Opal, "I can see you're starting to catch on. Now, your father, I wish I could get him to keep his shoes tied, too."

"Don't worry, Aunt Opal, he taught me everything I know...wait, I mean, yes, definitely, shoes tied."

Because it was nighttime, and for security reasons, all of the curtains were drawn.

"Your home is lovely," said Sarina as they all looked around at the nicely-furnished house. It was decorated with artifacts from all around the world.

"Thank you. Your parents all contacted me and said that you needed a safe place to stay and a chaperone," said Great Aunt Opal. "I'm so glad they called. You'll find two bedrooms made up for the girls upstairs, by my room, and two more bedrooms downstairs for the boys. And I have a surprise..."

A familiar face peeked from around the wall in the living room.

"Maria?" said Katrina and Sarina as they rushed forward to meet her. The princesses all hugged and began happily chatting, so grateful to see each other. Their friends, the Olsens, were there, too, and hugs went all around.

"How is your tooth, Maria," asked Sarina as they all sat down on the living room couches.

"Can you believe it?" said Maria. "I just had some meat between my teeth. The dentist was able to get it out."

"I'm glad it wasn't anything worse," said Katrina.

"By the time we got back to the safehouse at Lake Pinecone, after spending the day in town, we discovered you were missing," said Mrs. Olsen. "We immediately contacted security and your father. We were worried you had been kidnapped."

"We were following the message supposedly sent by you," said Sarina. "It had your secret code in it and everything."

"I know," said Mrs. Olsen. "We had the Wright cousins' parents investigate the matter to see if you'd made any contacts by phone and they discovered the text. It wasn't from us, believe me. Sarina, they said someone had hacked your phone and email accounts. The Wrights suggested we relocate here," said Mrs. Olsen.

"Then the message to meet you at the airport wasn't from you, either?" said Jonathan.

"No," said Mr. Olsen.

"And your great Aunt Opal has been so gracious to have us here," said Mrs. Olsen.

"The more the merrier," said Aunt Opal with a smile. "And since they've arrived, they've been so nice to talk to about nice places to visit around the world. Why, I haven't even needed to turn on the TV for background noise."

"Yes," said Maria, "and Sarina and Katrina, the beds here are good and bounceable—I mean—they're nice and soft."

The Olsens and Maria had retrieved Katrina and Sarina's things from the Lake Pinecone safehouse. Everyone slept well that night and finally had a good, sleep-in morning. Timothy and Maria were up, bright and early, though. They had Saturday morning cartoons to catch up on. After eating quick bowls of breakfast cereal in the dining room, they had called a cooties truce, placed the "can't cross over this line" pillow in the middle of the couch, and were enjoying the shows.

Later, great Aunt Opal served a more formal breakfast of orange juice, bacon, eggs, and banana pancakes topped with butter and homemade boysenberry syrup. It was delicious. Tim and Maria had even come back in for a moment to snitch some of the bacon.

After breakfast, the Wright cousins had a video meeting with their parents on Katrina's laptop computer. Their parents told them that Creepo and his gang had been rounded up and securely put in jail. When he was searched, the sheriff deputies found Sarina's phone in Creepo's back pocket. Creepo had evidently hacked the phone and used it to access Sarina's contacts and emails. According to a member of the gang, who briefly talked, Creepo was the one who had tricked the princesses into using the boat and later Jonathan about meeting the Olsens at the airport.

"Creepo's gang were after the large bounty on the princesses' heads," said Mr. Kevin Wright, Jonathan, Kimberly, and Tim's dad. "He and his henchmen were caught on surveillance camera and linked to a stolen boat at Lake Pinecone. They have a history of harming females. They're part of the scum of the earth who will do anything for money and power."

"They've done horrible things to you and the princesses," added his wife. "They're guilty of grand theft auto, assault with a deadly weapon, attempted murder...I'm just so grateful you're still alive. To protect innocent people, they must be put behind bars."

The subject turned to school.

"Because of the ongoing danger," said Mrs. Connie Wright, Lindy and Robert's mom, "you guys are going to have to do remote classes for a while. We've contacted your high school and they're setting it up."

"How long will that be?" asked Lindy.

"We don't know," Mrs. Wright replied. "That's being

assessed. We're just grateful that it's an option right now. Aunt Opal has graciously offered to host you all."

"Gladly," said Aunt Opal, "as long as needed."

The cousins worked on the details with their parents.

"What about our college chemistry class?" Tim asked his mom hopefully. "Has it been cancelled?"

His mom, Mrs. Rebecca Wright, smiled. "It has been changed—."

"Yippee!" shouted Tim.

"But unfortunately," said his dad, "the college has shifted you into a master's degree chemistry program."

"Masters?" said Tim. "That's above a bachelor's degree, isn't it?"

"Your father is just kidding," said Tim's mom. "Don't worry, you're only still in the third-year chemistry class. Your professor says he was so impressed by your and Robert's presentation that he couldn't bear to see you drop the class. He's set up a special program so you can do it all online. Oh, that and we also discovered that all five of you cousins somehow got enrolled in one of the college's marine biology classes."

"Marine biology?" said Lindy. "Come to think of it, that could be kind of fun."

"I agree," said Jonathan. "Sarina, maybe you and I could get in some more scuba diving."

"I'd love to," said Sarina with a grin. "But next time, I'll be sure and wear a wet suit."

"Wait just a minute," said Tim. "Couldn't we just catch some strange computer virus, maybe a wireless one, so we wouldn't have to do the classes at all?"

"Nice try," said Kimberly, "but you're not a computer."

"Okay, cinnamon rolls it is," said Robert.

"What?" said the rest of the group in unison.

"Chemistry class," Robert replied, "we can do cinnamon rolls for our next experiment."

"Cinnamon rolls?" said Tim with a smile. "This is going to be SWEET!"

Please Write a Review
Authors love hearing from their readers!

Please let Greg Smith know what you thought about this book by leaving a short review on Amazon or your other preferred online store. If you are under age 13, please ask an adult to help you. Your review will help other people find this fun and exciting adventure series!

To leave a review on Amazon, you can type in:
http://www.amazon.com/review/create-review?&asin=
B09WRPXPZY

Thank you!

Top tip: be sure not to give away any of the story's secrets!

About the Author

Greg, with palm trees in the background, exploring in the southern California desert. To learn and see more, visit GregoryOSmith.com.

Gregory O. Smith loves life! All of Greg's books are family friendly. He grew up in a family of four boys that rode horses, explored Old West gold mining ghost towns, and got to help drive an army tank across the Southern California desert in search of a crashed airplane!

Hamburgers are his all-time favorite food! (Hold the tomatoes and pickles, please.) Boysenberry pie topped with homemade vanilla ice cream is a close second. His current hobby is detective-like family history research.

Greg and his wife have raised five children and he now enjoys playing with his wonderful grandkids. He has been a Junior High School teacher and lived to tell about it. He has also been a water well driller, game and toy manufacturer, army mule mechanic, gold miner, railroad engineer, and living history adventure tour guide. (Think: dressing up as a Pilgrim, General George Washington, a wily Redcoat, or a California Gold Rush miner. Way too much fun!)

Greg's design and engineering background enables him to build things people can enjoy such as obstacle courses, waterwheels and ride-on railroads. His books are also fun filled, technically accurate, and STEM—Science, Technology, Engineering, and Math–supportive.

Greg likes visiting with his readers and hearing about their favorite characters and events in the books. To see the fun video trailers for the books and learn about the latest Wright cousin adventures, please visit **GregoryOSmith.com** today!

Enjoy every exciting book by award-winning author
Gregory O. Smith

The Wright Cousin Adventures series

1 The Treasure of the Lost Mine—Meet the five Wright cousins in their first big mystery together. I mean, what could be more fun than a treasure hunt with five crazy, daring, ingenious, funny and determined teenagers, right? The adventure grows as the cousins run headlong into vanishing trains, trap doors, haunted gold mines, and surprises at every turn!

2 Desert Jeepers—The five Wright cousins are having a blast 4-wheeling in the desert as they look for a long-lost Spanish treasure ship. And who wouldn't? There's so much to see! Palm trees, hidden treasure, UFO's, vanishing stagecoaches, incredible hot sauce, missing pilots. Wait! What?!

3 The Secret of the Lost City—A mysterious map holds the key to the location of an ancient treasure city. When the Wright cousins set out on horseback to find it, they run headlong into desert flash floods, treacherous passages, and formidable foes. Saddle up for thrilling discoveries and the cousins' wacky sense of humor in this grand Western adventure!

4 The Case of the Missing Princess—The Wright cousins are helping to restore a stone fort from the American Revolution. They expect hard work, but find more—secret passages, pirates, dangerous waterfalls, and a new girl with a fondness for swordplay. Join the cousins as they try to unravel this puzzling new mystery!

5   Secret Agents Don't Like Broccoli—The spy world will never be the same! Teenage cousins Robert and Tim Wright accidentally become America's top two secret agents—the notorious KIMOSOGGY and TORONTO. Their mission: rescue the beautiful Princess Katrina Straunsee and the mysterious, all-important Straunsee attaché case. They must not fail, for the future of America is in their hands. Get set for top secret fun and adventure as the Wright cousins outsmart the entire spy world—we hope!

6   The Great Submarine Adventure—The five Wright cousins have a submarine and they know how to use it! But the deeper they go, the more mysterious Lake Pinecone becomes. Something is wrecking boats on the lake and it's downright scary. Will the Wright cousins uncover the secret before they become the next victims? It's "up periscope" and "man the torpedoes" as the fun-loving Wright cousins dive into this exciting new adventure!

7   Take to the Skies—The five Wright cousins are searching for a missing airplane, but someone keeps sabotaging their efforts. Then a sudden lightning storm moves in and the mountains erupt into flames. The cousins must fly into action to rescue their friends. Will their old World War 2 seaplane hold together amidst the firestorms? Join the Wright cousins in this thrilling new aerial adventure!

8 The Wright Cousins Fly Again!—Secret bases, missing airplanes, and an unsolved World War 2 mystery are keeping the Wright cousins busy. During their research, the cousins discover a sinister secret lurking deep in Lake Pinecone, far more dangerous than they ever imagined. Will all their carefully made plans be wrecked? How will they survive? You'd better have a life preserver *and* a parachute ready for this fun and exciting new adventure!

9 Reach for the Stars—3-2-1-Blastoff! The Wright cousins are out of this world and so is the fun. Join the cousins as they travel into space aboard the new Stellar Spaceplane. Enjoy zero gravity and incredible views. But what about those space aliens Tim keeps seeing? The Wrights soon discover there really is something out there and it's downright scary. The cousins must pull together, with help from family and friends back on earth, if they are to survive. Can they do it?

10 The Sword of Sutherlee—These are dangerous times in the kingdom of Gütenberg. King Straunsee and his daughters have been made prisoners in their own castle. The five Wright cousins rush in to help. With secret passages and swords in hand, the cousins must scramble to rescue their friends and the kingdom. How will they do it?

11 The Secret of Trifid Castle—A redirected airline flight leads the Wright cousins back into adventure: mysterious luggage, racing rental cars, cool spy gear, secret bunkers, and menacing foes. Lives hang in the balance. Who can they trust? Join the Wright cousins on a secret mission in this fun, daring, and exciting new adventure!

 **12 The Clue in the Missing Plane**— A cold war is about to turn hot in the Kingdom of Gütenberg. Snowstorms, jagged mountains, enemy soldiers. Can the Wright cousins discover the top secret device before it's too late?

 13 The Wright Disguise—It's the Wright Cousins' 13th adventure, so what could go wrong, Wright...write...rite...right? Uh-oh, I think we're in serious trouble!

The Wright cousins are back in America and diving into their active life of crazy inventions, school classroom mix-ups, and paintball battles. But their visiting friends, Sarina and Katrina, run into trouble: their royal anonymity is compromised by a story gone viral. A treacherous enemy has now placed a bounty on their heads. The Wright Cousins must drop everything and spring into action. How will they save their friends?

 **14 The Mystery of Treasure Bay**—The Wright Cousins are traveling to the beautifully lush tropical Island of Talofa. There's so much to do: boogie boarding, scuba diving, exploring, boating, and surfing. But they also encounter danger lurking in the deep ocean waters.

With fierce storms, spooky lighthouses, sinister traps, and menacing foes, how will the Wright Cousins unravel the puzzling mysteries before them?

15 The Secret of the Sunken Ship— Anyone up for a dive? This fun and exciting sequel to book #14 finds the Wright cousins searching Talofa and its neighboring tropical islands for a mysterious lost treasure. Along with amazing underwater discoveries, the Wright's and their friends face confusing clues, eerie secret caves, and a desperate gang who will stop at nothing to steal the treasure out from under them. How will the Wright cousins survive the danger and surprises that await them?

Additional Books by Gregory O. Smith

The Hat, George Washington, and Me!— Part time travel, part crazy school, totally fun. "Hey Mom, there's a patriot in my cereal box!" When a mysterious package arrives in the mail with a tricorn hat and toy soldiers inside, fourteen-year-old Daniel, of course, tries on the hat. Now he's in for it because the hat won't come off and he must wear the hat to school!

Daniel suddenly finds himself up against classroom bullies, real Redcoats pounding on the schoolroom door, and his life turned upside down. Is his American history report really coming to life?

Rheebakken 2: Last Stand for Freedom—"This action-packed novel launches readers directly into the fray on the first page and does not let go until the story's conclusion."—*Riverdancer.* The freedom of the entire world is at stake, and it's up to one man to preserve that freedom—no matter the cost. Fighter pilot Eric Brown has been tasked with the top secret mission of ferrying King Straunsee and his daughter

Allesandra to safety in the United States. Unfortunately, there are many others who would choose to see the monarch destroyed rather than permitting him to secure global freedom.

This is a fast-paced, action-centered story that will appeal to teen and young adult readers who appreciate military stories with a wholesome approach.

 Strength of the Mountains: A Wilderness Survival Adventure—Matt and his relatives are going balloon camping. The morning arrives. The balloon is filled. An unexpected storm strikes. Matt, all alone, is swept off into the wilderness in an unfinished balloon. Totally lost, what will he find? How will he survive? Will he ever make it home again? Join Matt in this heartwarming story about wilderness survival and friendship.

 Wright Cousin Adventures #1 Fun Cookbook ~ 50 Favorite Desserts You'll Love to Make, Bake, Eat, and Share! Each delicious dessert recipe includes easy-to-follow directions and author Lisa's helpful and unique, _hand-drawn illustrations._ You'll also find classic Wright Cousin humor, puzzles, secret codes, _and_ clues to Tim Wright's "Top Secret Recipe" hidden somewhere inside the cookbook. Includes Delicious Cookies, Brownies & Bars, Candy & Popcorn, Ice Cream Treats, Cakes & Sweet Breads, and Refreshingly Fun Drinks. Delight your family and friends today with a sweet surprise from the _#1 Fun Cookbook!_

Please tell your family and friends about these fun and exciting new adventures so they can enjoy them too! Help spread the word!

Sign up for the latest adventures at GregoryOSmith.com

https://gregoryosmith.com/

Made in the USA
Las Vegas, NV
08 December 2024

12928729R00083